u.v.ray was born in Birmingham, England
in 1967.

His work has appeared in numerous
magazines and anthologies
around the world.

Also by u.v.ray on Murder Slim Press:
*Spiral Out*
*We Are Glass*
*The Migrant*
*Black Cradle*

He lives in Staffordshire and runs his own
book and vinyl record stall, Outlaw Books.

# DRUG STORY

Copyright © 2019 u.v.ray
All rights reserved
ISBN: 9781097788064

*Drug Story* is presented as a work of fiction and any likeness to any person living or dead is entirely coincidental.

10 9 8 7 6 5 4 3 2 1
First Printing

Cover © 2019 u.v.ray
Design and Editing © 2019 Steve Hussy

No part of this book may be used or reproduced in any manner whatsoever without written permission from the publisher, except in the case of quotations embodied in critical articles and reviews.

For all queries contact:
Murder Slim Press, 22 Bridge Meadow, Hemsby, Norfolk. NR29 4NE United Kingdom

Published by Murder Slim Press 2019
www.murderslim.com

# **drug story**
## *a novel*

*this system's gonna fall soon, to an angry young tune
and that's a concrete cold fact.
- Sixto Rodriguez*

## Prologue

i come to my senses shivering in the cold night silence, starin throo yellery eyes an i've bin blowin shit up my nose for the last 5 years or more, waitin for the inevitable, an i've not just got a broken face i got a broken soul. life had bin nuthin to me for Christ knows how long, nuthin but endless mind-numbing teevee an chronic masturbation to alleviate the desperate tedium of the dripping hours an dripping days an dripping years w/no pleasure in life no more, it's just the involuntary ejaculation of the hanged man.

i am alone in the world an i'm sweating out a fever like i got sumthin crawlin beneath my skin an though i'm not exactly loused i got the dart still stickin out my wrist, i torn the vein an it's comin out a me like the blud a fuckin Christ on the cross. bombed out my head i wake up slumped at the wheel a the hired Dodge pick-up skidded to a halt in a ditch by the side a the road on the *110* comin west or east or north i dunno which way from Pasadena, just outside a Los Angeles. i flick on the interior light. my watch says 2:10 a.m. dash lights burnin red, i fire her up an pull back onto the freeway, tyres peelin all over the road. radio tuned to 95.5 KLOS FM, dj crankin out Mudhoney's *Touch Me I'm Sick* an i'm all out a donkey an all i am thinkin about is where the fuck i'm gonna score some more an now the hire company gonna be tryna sting me like a 1000 $$ or sumthin stupid for the scratches running right down the passenger side a the Dakota V6. i turn the radio right up an stare transfixed out the windscreen dead ahead, big city lights sparklin like diamonds in the distant night.

    it's May 1990 an last 3 months i bin workin illegally, sum shit job at sum orange farm in Redlands, just kinda east of L.A, picking oranges, just tryna scrape together enough cash-in-hand for a plane ticket home to get away from this insane goth chick called Lilian. Lilian was originally from sum where in San Fran, who i'd met an ended up shacked up together in East Hollywood in a rental on Yucca Street, couple a blocks away from the Capitol Records building while she was in Hollywood waitin tables at the Blue Monkey bar an dreamin of movie stardom like just about every other girl waitin tables in Hollywood. she was totally mad, always accusing me of completely off the wall stuff. 1 of her best ones was accusing me of trying to put thoughts in her head.

half the street was a building site, with signs up offering luxury accommodation in Spanish villa style apartments. Lilian had black hair down to her waist an despite the fact she looked like Vampira an i was gettin sucked-off to death, she was kind a skinny an all body dismorphic fucked-up in the head an wound up 1 day up on the roof garden a the apartment in the blazin California sun cranked up to the max on sum shit or other, havin another 1 of her freak-outs, the mad bitch screamin she wuz gonna jump. an the thing was the stupid bitch probably wouldn't have even killed herself, she'd a just busted her legs or sumthin stupid.

i wasn't gonna fuck around no more, i was just about done, man. i walked out a there an carried on walkin.

after spending 3 days sobering up in a shuttered motel room just off the *405* i abandoned the damaged Dodge in the motel parking lot an cabbed it over to LAX at 5 a.m on a clear blue-skied Monday morning.

my flight home was at 10.

# 1

i never usually know what day it is. i navigate time by gig dates on my tickets. right now i'm lit up like fuckin gelignite. i'm at a party at sum body's house an i don't even know whose house it is or where it is or how i got here an the DJ's blastin out Led Zeppelin's *Communication Breakdown*. still got the ticket in my pocket cuz i ain't even bin home yet. it's August 22nd, 1991 an last night i was at the Mudhoney/Hole gig at Goldwyn's on Suffolk Place an i wish i could remember more about it but everything is a blur an i barely remember nuthin w/all the whiskey an speed pulsing throo my blood an permeating my muscles an sinew.

the smoke machines are pumpin out clouds a rollin fog an derz a black girl layed out on the kitchen table gettin finger-raped. she's mostly naked, tits exposed, skirt up around her waist, bunch a dumb-looking, dipshit grunge rock kids standin around watching an sum gimp in a Monochrome Set tshirt got his fingers pushed in her cunt an he's ramming them in hard but she don't move at all she's like comatose an then i see the empty bottle a spirits on the floor an the makeshift disco lights propped up all over the place are goin blam blam blam blam like gun shots in my eyes while sum other wasted kid leans into me, he looks outta place like he's just sum college disco type in a Liverpool football shirt, you know his eyes all wide like he's absorbing the whole scene, but he's like twenny yrs old or sumthin, a skeletal pale face smokin a cigarette an he's got the shoulder length wavy brown hair as if he thinks he's Jim fuckin Morrison or sum one, acting all languid an detached cuz he's on sum chickenshit lizard-king trip. an the kid is absolutely pissed up out his fuckin face an he goes: "i been there like that though, know what i mean? i mean you get a girl, man, an she just lies there an lets you do it. an you don't even think about it at the time but you kinda know she's not really into it but she just lies there an let's you do it anyway. she just lies there an totally let's you do it an next day bitch calls it rape."

i don't even know what this douche-bag college kid's talkin about all i can really hear when he opens his mouth is wah wah wah wah wah, i mean this kid's a real dipshit but i just nod an repeat "yeah yeah, they just lie there an let you do it" an then i walk away w/my empty glass back to the cabinet where they keep the drinks to reload.

i snorted a couple a rails w/my girlfriend Amy in the bedroom earlier an i've definitely reached escape velocity. i use the term girlfriend loosely but whatever she is to me, now i've gone an lost her sum where an it don't even occur to me that the piece of bar-room trash that she is mighta fucked off sum where w/sum fuckin guy as per her usual m.o an like a dweeb i'm wandering about the crowds a people from room to room in this huge Victorian 3 storey town-house so blitzed i feel like i'm strung out across the heavens an i could crush the gods themselves between my hands.

\* \* \*

everythin is a haze an i don't remember leaving the house an when i do i'm so wrecked i don't even recognise what district i'm in, sumwhere up Handsworth. but i remember the ride home. kind of. bits of it anyway. sitting alone in back a the taxi an still totally fuckin wired, lookin out the rear winnder like i'm seeing the world in cinemascope w/everything spinning round me like a grainy video tape running on >>FF. the deserted streets all grey an cold, an all pervading sense of everything colliding w/the moon beautiful an massive, hanging low on the horizon like a pale blue skull between the angular tower blocks an the haze of orange phosphorescent street lights reflected on the glistening wet streets as dark clouds drift across a fathomless sky in their irreversible succession.

we stop at sum red lights where on the corner there's sum kinda whore-drama going on, a whole bunch a dime-store hookers all screamin an bitchin at each other an they're all decked out in their high heels an hotpants an big hair like bitches in heat an i'm thinking to myself they don't look half bad. but they're all screamin an shoutin an i turn to the driver an i go: "what the holy fuckadoodle is goin on here, man?" an the muslim taxi driver in his little white cap turns in his seat an says: "you stay away from them type a dirty girls, you know? they're bad, man. bad bad girls, eh?" he points down at my crotch an says, "you wanna ketch sum bad thing down there, eh? ha ha ha... you wanna ketch crabs, eh? you stay away from them girls." an then the traffic light changes to green an he shakes his head an half smiles at their antics an goes tut tut tut w/his tongue as we pull away. it starts raining an he switches the windscreen wipers on an i am hypnotised by their back an forth motion as we shift throo the empty night.

but i am the lonliest man in the world, i am the one you will see in the cafés staring into his coffee or up at the sky, i'll be watching all the people go by w/their expressionless faces, disengaged from my surroundings. but it's all just images. images are everything. i watch not like a human being but like a Super 8, capturing tiny moments in time, replaying the f-l-i-c-k-e-r-i-n-g images in my mind over an over, trying to make sense of the world. an so far i can't make none at all.

driver got the radio on, sum obscure channel or other, i don't understand the constant babble, they're talking in Urdu or sum such language an there's no music, it just sounds like a 100 voices all jabbering at once even though there's only probably 4 of em. driver turns to face me again an waves a weary hand at the radio an sez: "ahh, they're saying Britain is a bastard becuz every time there is conflict between India an Pakistan both countries buy weapons from UK." i'm not really interested in all that politics stuff but i reply gleefully anyway: "hey, they can't say things like that in this country can they?" an the driver eyes me in his rear view mirror an laughs, "same in any country, man. you can say what you like... as long as it's what they want you to say."

driver flicks over the channel an there's about 5 seconds of *Should I Stay Or Should I Go* by the Clash before he knocks the radio off altogether.

"see, here you got your black people," the driver says. "nobody likes them, right? me, i'm from Pakistan. if i go to India they think i'm a nigger. over there, Pakistanis are treated like niggers. customer i had in my cab other day was from Estonia, she told me Russians are their niggers. every society got to have sum body to call nigger. makes them feel better about themselves, you know what am saying?"

it's abysmally sad that most people's lives amount to nuthin. eat sleep fuck piss talk. mostly talk. an they talk shit. their lives don't mean anything, their whole existence is nuthin more than a fleeting anomaly on a radar screen sum where. that's all everyone does, eat sleep fuck piss talk. but mostly talk. everybody's so fulla shit an in the end people always lose. in the end people always lose everything becuz their lives are hopeless an they're all so stupid they swallowed all the bullshit that's been shovelled to them. but there are no empirical truths, an every human thought, every ideology is flawed sum where, sum how. we are each of us alone, no one truly knows anyone else an becuz we are all egocentric we're all always talking about different things an simply assuming we understand each other.

"yeah, the Jews daynt kill no Jesus," i tell the driver, "it was the blacks." an he looks an he laughs an sez, "nah, nah the blacks didn't kill him. but you get what am sayin, brutha. you get what am sayin." an he stares at me in his mirror an goes: "i like you, kid. i like the cut of your jib."

"yeah," i say. "our drums are beatin to the same tune."

we head towards the city centre, faux glamour of the city lights reflecting across the dark windscreen like sum kinda strange an beautiful bright night flowers.

\* \* \*

must a got home totally zonked out bout like 4 a.m. i wake up at like 1 in the afternoon an fumble around in the bed for the bottle of whisky that i passed out drinkin, it's poured out all over the bedsheets an the place stinks a whisky fumes. haul myself outta bed w/a face like Mick Hucknall eating a jar of Swarfega. hard reality of hitting baseline now, muscles all stiff like rigor mortis is prematurely setting in to my living tissue, an i go to the bathroom to douse my face in cold water to try an assuage the hypersomnia an derz blud in the basin all pretty bright red against the white porcelain an i mean like a load of it like sum body's throat bin cut but i got no idea where it's come from till i look in the mirror an see the congealed blud round my mouth an realise i've coughed all that shit up w/no recollection of doing it. i'm as good as dead, no feelings left for anyone or anything, just a dead-eyed stare in the mirror. i go to the refrigerator an get a can a Coca-Cola. ice cold an oil-slick black, effervescent on the tongue. euphoria.

i live in a flat above a closed down take-away joint called the Pilot Burger Bar on Hill Street an i can hear the rain against the winnder above the constant throb of traffic an trains makin that slow laborious clatter in an outta New Street Station. resounding noize of police sirens. same cycle of events every day, the whole city like a clockwork toy or as if we all got a script to read an we're all just riding the carousel round an round an i feel like i'm crashed back down in a world that don't really fucking exist. none of it seems real to me, seems like everything just runs on automatic an 1 day i will be gone but the circus will simply carry on an on, an endless amorphous shifting mass of meaninglessness.

setting aside moral or political leanings, setting aside your learned moral indoctrinations, notions of right an wrong, i am more interested in how an why human minds come to fruition in the universe - an it don't matter if it is the mind of Hitler or the mind of Henry Kissinger or the mind of Leo Baekeland or the mind of Philo Farnsworth or anybody else that changed the world - an how those minds dissipate again. i wonder how all our minds slot into the supreme universal mechanism.

i pick up the phone, try to call Amy but there's no answer so i roll back into bed feelin like i could sleep for a 1000 years, wanting to wake up in a different time an a different world.

\* \* \*

at about 4 p.m, i slot an old porno tape in the Panasonic vhs player an ff>> it past all the credits. i sit on the sofa an stare at the pieces of flesh shifting about the screen like little string puppets. premise is this: blonde in black catsuit is sum kind of assassin. she's come down the building on ropes, prized open the winnder an climbed into this hotel bedroom where this guy is sleeping. as far as porn goes, this is big budget shit. she's sposed to kill this guy but she pulls back the bedsheets, Beretta M9 held in her hand, an sees his cock an whimpers "oh my god, it's so big." she drops the gun an falls to her knees in worship an takes the vile lookin oiled-up thing in her mouth. there's sum kinda camera triggercut an next thing you know she's out of all her clothes an the guy flips her down on the bed an fucks her senseless / another triggercut / an sum other naked girl, a skinny freakish brunette w/big fake bazooka tits comes outta nowhere, prob from behind the camera or sum shit an starts watching what's going on an she leans against the doorframe, lickin her lips an rubbing her clit, going: "oh...oh...oh my pussy is so wet."

they're all talking this synthetic rhetoric shit like oh yeah fuck that pussy, fuck my tight little pussy an like oh yeah baby suck that cock an the assassin is sucking the guy's cock again as he stretches out on the bed gettin ready to deliver the big-ass money shot. she opens her mouth - rocket-red lipstick lips - an tells him: "gimme yr cum, spray me w/yr cum hmm oh yeah i wanna taste yr cum" as he masturbates in her face. he grabs her hair an violently yanks her head back hard an says "open yr fucking mouth here it comes ya little bitch" an then smooth jazz muzak kicks in, killin the scene like you're in an elevator or hanging on the telephone on hold to British Gas an the assassin sticks out her tongue an licks his cock an takes the blast of cum in her mouth an in her hair an she rubs it on her tits, her body jerking as the brunette pounds her from behind w/a massive veiny pinkflesh strap-on that she musta pulled out her ass or sum-fucking-where becuz it was nowhere to be seen before. she pounds away w/the strap-on yelling "yeah yeah yeah yeah" until the assassin screams "i'm coming" an collapses, pussysquirting what's clearly piss all over the guy who lies there an takes it, going in a deep, thick voice: "oh fuck yeah gimme yer juices, bay-beee."

    i haven't even managed to masturbate, i've fallen asleep on the sofa when i'm woken up by the phone. it's gone dark an i turn on the table lamp an extinguish the cigarette i've dropped on the carpet in the ashtray. i pick up the cordless handset an walk over to the winnder thinking it must be Amy as i press it to my ear. pasted on the billboard across the street above the NCP carpark is sum army recruitment ad that's got a picture of a soldier in full battle dress takin aim w/a rifle an it says: …**OR PERHAPS YOU FIND A NIGHT IN FRONT OF THE TV MORE EXCITING?** over which sum commie pinko bastard grafittied in black spray paint:

Ⓐ **aristocracies have to convince us war is glorious because they expect us to die protecting their finances** Ⓐ

an then in big red letters sum body else added: **YOU GOTTA FIGHT FOR YOUR RIGHT TO PAAAARTY!!!**

but it ain't Amy, it's Superfast on the line an he says, "glue yourself together, gringo. i'll be round in bout twenny minutes."

an that is that. click. he puts the phone down.

## 2

of course, sum people wonder why i live the life i do. an if i'm asked i tell them i'm really just the same as anybody else an i didn't really have a choice. circumstances beyond our control shape us. i was born in 1967 an my 17 yr old mother died of a brain tumour when i was 6 months old. i never knew her. i don't even know what she looked like, ain't even ever seen a photograph. for the first few years a my life i endured a timeless, abstract subsistence in a bleak old red brick victorian-era built welfare orphanage just outside Birmingham City, was passed around different homes for a while before being settled w/relatively wealthy adoptive parents an aquired an incurably unhappy, mentally unstable an perpetually depressed mother dosed up to her eyeballs on valium most of her life. i've seen all the religious histrionics. beat me black an blue sum times, an then i'd watch as she collapsed to her knees, sobbing uncontrollably, begging god for forgiveness for the things i'd made her do. she prayed like that while i bled in the corner. i knew from the age a ten i was on my own in this world. an truth is i wouldn't want it any other way, i don't wanna be part of any group, i am not 1 of you, i take my knocks an i keep getting up again, no one ever gonna keep me down.

i am now just about to hit 25 years old. my birth name was Mark Costine an that is the name i have reverted to using but truth is you could call me by any name. everythin is empty an everythin is broken an when you see me you will sense no gravity about me, you might think it's like looking at a synthesized image of sum one on a television screen. an i don't know what to say it's like but best way to describe it is that Mark Costine moved outta his body a long time ago an sum thing else moved in. i'm all fucked up. a fragment broken off the body of humanity.

i am the lonely man you see in the cafés

like sum fucking thing gone wrong w/the straggly J. Mascis hair an Kohl eye-liner. i am the alien absolved of all connection w/the human race. i am alone in the world like my flesh an bones are made a stone. i don't know where i come from or who i am. i can sense death coming, a life passing without meaning or event, i am sumthin ugly, a life waiting to be anulled, living an existence of slow, induced suicide, like those days when all you want to do is bloody your head against a wall becuz it feels better than the incessant numbness of existence.

# 3

Superfast's this skinny to fuck speedfreak. that's why he's called Superfast. but truth be told he'll neck any kinda drugs really, uppers, downers, he don't care at all. he's also totally paranoid about the food he reckons they're giving us. he's kind of a dork an makes no real contribution to the human race. known him bout a year now, met him at the Jane's Addiction gig at the Institute in '90 sum time an i dunno if you'd really call it a friendship but we struck sum kind a connection like speedfreaks do. this one time we were dossing about on the sofa round his gaff, havin a toke a the old la-buena to assuage the effects of a 2 day speed binge, an he was telling me he'd been reading up on this genetically modified foods shit they're gonna be growing in a few years. bananas that aint bananas at all, they're man-made. he spends his time studying all this kind a crap. an he talks a lot a crap, too. all food, Superfast sed, in the end is gonna be man-made an fulla cancer causing crystals. it's coming big style, he reckons, yielding greater profits for farmers an nuthin but death an sickness for us all. "another 10 years an you wone even know about it, they'll slip it all in on the quiet. they'll have us eatin shit an we wone even know it."

his shitbox old v-dub camper pulls up an parks half on the pavement on the double yellers outside my Hill Street flat, he leaves his blinkers going. although the Pilot Burger joint's all closed down an boarded up, the entrance to my flat above is still throo the dilapidated dust laden shop so i go down an let him in an he comes up the flat buzzing on cigarettes an Pro-Plus. he got his Birmingham City football scarf wrapped round his neck an he comes in rubbin his hands together an says "well, we stuffed Bury on Saturday dae we?" i remind him i don't follow football. Superfast's face is always like it's contorted, like he's in sum kinda constant inner anguish, i expect all Birmingham City FC fans look like that. there's sum thing to do w/an old Gypsy curse on their stadium that appears to be working its black magic on them all. sum old story about how they turfed an old gypsy woman in a caravan off the land so they could build the football ground an she cursed the club for as long as it stayed there.

Pro-Plus are these little energy pills you can buy over the counter at the pharmacy that students pop to help get throo their exams. pep pills they call them an they got this super strength nuclear grade caffeine in them so one tab is like 10 cups a coffee or sumthin stupid an if you swallow enough of them you're sposed to get a buzz but i tried that shit once, i bombed down 25 or sum thing stupid an all they did was make me feel kinda dizzy an sick.

today Superfast got his faux gold dime-store sunglasses on. thinks he's Elvis Presley. but he's bin pretty ill recently, tho it's nuthin more complicated than calcium deficiency due to excessive amphetamine consumption, he lives on a constant diet of nuclear grade teevee dinners an amphetamines - his fucking teeth are falling out an his hair is like dry as straw, he's breaking out in scabs. but he takes anythin he can get his hands on an the doc's also had him on the Dollie for the last 5 months cuz of his skag addiction an by the grey/yeller look a the scabby mutant i reckon his liver function is all fucked up.

but Superfast's telling himself a story, man;

he thinks it's sum thing "they're" slipping him an he's also concerned becuz his doctor is from Guatemala or sum place. "yeah yeah," Superfast expatiates, "i'm gonna end up dyin cuz sum 3rd world fuckin witch-doctor is gonna diagnose me w/sum mumbo-jumbo sickness. he's gonna be like: yeah, you got devils in your blud an you gotta eat this scorpion under a full moon to get em back out again. an Superfast does his approximation of an African accent: "Oooh yeh. dem is de worse case a devils in de blud i evva see! you weet fo de nex full moon an you eat dis scorpion ay gonna gives you. tank ya verrrry much - das wan hundred an fiffy punds pliz."

"an you know my answer to that?" Superfast says, flicking a thumb over his shoulder, "back to de plantations, boi."

Jesus H.

i pour us sum coffees an we sit down on the sofa. i'm distracted for a second by the teevee, i dunno why my attention is taken but the news is sayin sum thing about the civil war in Yugoslavia. They sez cluster bombs have killed 50,000 so far already.
50,000. really? wow.
sounds like a bit a bullshit propaganda to me. you just gotta watch out for anything they try to tell you on the box.

"i'm all outta the old white lightning," Superfast says. "an deez Pro-Plus ain't cuttin the mustard. any chance i can nab 3 wraps of your finest, gringo?"

i eyeball him playfully right throo his sunglasses, rub my fingertips together an tell him: "price is a tenner each. providing you got the lettuce, bruv, you can have what you like." i have to check cuz Superfast ain't usually got the moolah. he's full a shit an he needs to go for colonic irrigation or whatever it is they call it when they clean all the shit outta you, they need to suck it all outta him an stop all the crap that rises up an spews out his mouth. but sum times you detect that metallic smell about him, you know. i think he gets his paranoid delusions from smoking crystal meth.

he's also a con man. no idea how he does his shit but he sells famous people's autographs on the flea-market 2 days a week. Marilyn Monroe, Muhammad Ali, Paul McCartney. he's got em all. that's pretty much how he earns his wedge, man. but the autographs are all fakes. he's got a pro lookin set-up at his stall but he forges them all hisself, certs of authenticity an all, the whole sheboodle. but i mean, you'd take one look at this kid an you wouldn't buy jack-shit off him. which is obviously why he's usually broke. but even as a low-life fraudster he way over-values his own worth, i mean he thinks he's Birmingham's answer to Yellow Kid Weil or sum one.

"yeah yeah don't worry," Superfast goes. "i got the lettuce." an he hands me thirty quid for 3 wraps an i give him the 3 little paper envelopes, pulling them outta the breast pocket of my denim jacket.

"...an by the way, Guatemala ain't in Africa," i tell him, "it's in central America you fuckin mutant... where half this shit comes from."

it's raining now an it beats against the winnder, it kinda looks a dirty petrol colour from all the exhaust fumes an Superfast looks at it spuriously. his big eyebrows are moving up an down like Animal off the Muppets an the words come outta his mouth like he ain't even thinkin bout what he's sayin: "that ain't no normal rain, man. that's sumthin the government is spraying us with."

# 4

one a those mornings when the sun comes up an hits the buildings bathing them in beautiful golden glow. i'm watching the riots on teevee that are happening right now just a couple a miles away cross the city in Handsworth. they say a fuckin power-cut caused a blackout during the night, sparking off a loada looting in what i call the African Quarter of the city. they're robbin shops an stealin cars, wanging molotovs at police riot vans that explode an dissipate against the armoured vehicles w/no visible harm done an police responding by charging in an beatin the fuckers down like dogs. the streets are on fire an the teevee reporter is referring to the rioters as West Indian youths, sayin sum shit about they're gonna bring in the army w/armoured cars an water cannons an rubber bullets before it gets as bad as it did in '85 the last time it all kicked off. in '85 it all started w/a cop giving sum guy a parking ticket outside the Acapulco Café on Lozells Road, an that sparked off 3 days a riots an lootin an everything burnin like a war-zone an people started gettin killed, whole buildings wiped off the map.

now they got this old fuck white ass resident on the screen an he's calling the rioters the scum a the earth an sayin they should be shot like rats. behind him they turn a car on its roof an set fire to it an a police unit moves in w/shields an batons. the guy they're interviewing turns an watches an then turns back to the camera waving his arms about erratically an says: "see? see? don't get mad just cuz i told the truth." an just then not 2 blocks away derz the crack a gun shots.

they say sum one walked into the Red Lion pub on the Soho Road an told everyone a teenage black girl got raped by sum white kids. they sed she was in an alleyway when it happened, her cries muffled by a scarf wrapped round her face. but maybe they got that wrong cuz i saw what happened in that house. maybe that was the girl an maybe it wasn't, maybe sum shit like that went down sum where or other or maybe it's all just a lot a crap an no black girl got raped at all. nobody on teevee knows who she is or where she is or who or where the white kids are either. nobody knows jack shit cept a black girl got raped an the cops don't wanna do nuthin about it, even tho sum body sed they found the discarded scarf they sed was used to muffle her cries an that's why the riots really happened -- an not cuz a the power cut -- but becuz sum body found the scarf an they sed she was muffled w/it an now it's like hysteria spreadin throo the streets but it's all bullcrap anyway becuz these fuckers don't truly care if sum girl got raped or not it's just an excuse to grab sum loot.

    it's all conjecture. people are full a shit, man. they're just robbing all this shit cuz they think havin stuff raises their social value an they're too stupid to know money is an illusion. it's like the gov prints particular images onto pieces of paper an tells us it's worth such-an-such amount. they print their own money, but you're not allowed to print yours, you gotta slave away to earn sum a their legal variety but it's never yours in any case, it's just a loan an in the end throo forced taxation, which is really just point blank extortion, all money gravitates back into the corporate machine. but anyway, you're standing there w/a £10 note in your pocket but what the fuck all you got is the government's word for it that it's worth £10 an if you just accept what they say that makes you a good citizen. it's all goddamn bullshit. your only intrinsic worth is based on how much money you generate for the government. to them your only name is your tax number. but these people are lootin these shops, man, loadin up their stash in salvaged shopping trolleys an then gettin mugged themselves tryin to haul all the shit home.

no matter what they say society is self-regulating, so you can save all your white tears of guilt cuz on the teevee right now as far as i can see it's black shoot black. it's like they bin coerced, socially engineered, into sum kind a ideological civil war amongst themselves. an i think they probably have. the order of things gotta keep these people down an the easiest way to do that is decimate their social cohesion, which ain't exactly difficult since people's most enduring relationships in the first place these days is w/the characters they watch on teevee in the soap operas. but truth is they gotta get you turning on each other. what we need is people like the IRA an they need to start puttin bullets in a few politicians instead a people on the street.

the streets are at boiling point. reducing down. an in the end everythin gets reduced down to the lowest common denominator, boiled down to its most basic ingredients. it's the 3rd fuckin world out there on the streets.

most a the street-trash, the social an genetic underclass, are runnin about like headless chickens shoutin fuck the pigs, fuck the pigs an throwin half-enders or anythin else they can get their angry hands on, but the more intelligent rioters have organised their own kinda battalions, commissioned their own colonels directing them to attack the police in waves, but still achieving nuthin but getting beaten down. there's priests an shit out there from the churches tryin to assuage the situation w/their megaphones of diplomacy but no body takes a bit a notice as the contagion further spreads like lymphoma becuz in the heat of the moment these ineffectual morons think they're in the middle a sum kind a revolution. they think they're gonna change sumthin. but nuthin ever gonna change.

people squeal like pigs for equality cuz they just don't know that inequality is an ordinary phenomenon in nature. in our fabricated human society equality must be enforced by strict political regulation of people's thoughts an behaviour. but political parties are just committees that act in unison, so the surreptitious devises of each individual politician can be obfuscated, as if on appointment of the nation they have acted on behalf of the people as one inclusive mass. but it's all bullshit becuz the real purpose of government is to crystalise your vision of authority so that you live in subordination. an you can't cherry pick which areas of life you think this so-called equality should apply to. truth is, if equality was a natural phenomenon it wouldn't have to be politically enforced.

that's how it works, most a the time anyway. but occasionally sum body who hasn't swallowed the bullshit comes along an sticks a fuckin well-deserved bullet in one a their heads.

do not concern yourselves with politics. politics is the manifestation of man's parochial ideologies, his failure to comprehend the true potential of the human race. politics is small thought, it is the petulant language of the slave. in all its persuasions politics is the most hideous an debilitating ideology of all human constructs, a system that facilitates the destruction of the true genius that dwells within the human mind. we become as diminshed gods, emaciated by trivialities.

but you look around at everyone, man, an it's like they just got this bewildered expression on their faces, like they got question marks in their eyes, like they just can't make no sense of life at all. they bin brutalised. an you can't kill it. you can't kill it becuz it's sumthin inside us. it's sumthin inside ourselves an we establish sum system a thought on which we can all agree but then sure enough we begin dividing an fighting again. dividing an fighting. dividing an fighting. it's a constant. an i don't have all the answers but i'll tell you this: if we're ever gonna get anywhere we havta kill politics as a system a thought.

yeah, yeah. every now an then you get your counter-cultures, like the hippies or the punks. an it all seems like it's heading sum where big - i mean you're gonna bring the system down, man. but they just move the corporations in an disempower it in a flanking maneuver, commercialise it, turn it all into sum asinine fashion statement. they take punk out the back street clubs an put it on *Top of the Pops.* they start selling Sex Pistols tshirts in Tesco. an just like that they fuck you over every single time an people are just too stupid to see what's really goin on.

i mix myself a Moscow Mule to bomb a gram a the speed down with an i turn down the sound on the teevee an put the stereo on an sprawl on the sofa watching the action to the Stooges *I Gotta Right* thwacking out the speakers an now it's like watchin a film cept for the fact that outside i can hear the constant stream of police sirens as every available unit goes racing throo the veins a the city towards the affected area like white blood cells systemically programmed to fight an infection.

# 5

the kid's got Hollywood looks. that is to say, he looks like sum freak out a horror film. it's Saturday night an i'm at Loaded, sittin on the sofas in the murky subterranean downstairs bar near the bubble wall an the dj's blastin out the Mary Chain's *Blues From a Gun* an it sounds to me like he's speeded it up a touch too an the strobe lights flashin in sync w/the thwacking bass drum are hittin me like hammer blows an everyone moving around me in thrilling staccato machine gun images. the weazelesque kid all burned out, lookin at me w/these small blue kerosene eyes is reclined on the sofa next to me, he grabs my arm an shouts in my ear: "shit me, this record is fuckin ace! who is it, man?" an i suck on my Marlboro, take a sip a my Corona an tell him this is the Jesus an fuckin Mary Chain, kid. the kid shakes my hand, introduces himself, tells me he's called Crow an then he adds: "no homo, man. me girlfriend just gone to the bar."

shit, i can't believe how ugly this kid is. an he ain't ugly by sum unfortunate accident either, like he's bin in a car wreck or sum thing. w/his gnarled, lopsided features an hare-lip poor bastard looks like sum thing genetically went wrong when he was first formed in the womb. born ugly. a real fuckin scornful dweeb an you only have to look at this kid to know he's the kind a mutant that wipes his ass from the back to the front.

an then i see her. Amy. she appears out the darkness an comes gliding throo the clouds a dry ice like a cyclone towards me. she's carrying drinks an wearing a short gold dress an pink Converse All-Stars an she comes over an instead sits on the hybrid's lap, puts her arms around his neck still holding their drinks an kisses him. the kid don't amount to much an i wonder if he don't realise wearing a Styx tshirt might incite others to punch him in the face. Amy ain't even noticed me, don't even know i'm in the place, an then she sees me an leaps back up an throws her long red hair back an gives me the big blue eyes an says, surprised: "Mark? ... ... oh..." an me an the kid look at each other for a few seconds an then i shrug smokin my cigarette an say to him: "your girlfriend, eh? well, Crow, it seems you an i are practically related." Amy glares at me an goes condescendingly: "oh, you horrid pig."

man, this girl got sum gall, i tell you. i dunno what story she keeps telling herself but she always takes the higher ground in all matters. "oh, fuckin yeah," i nod an laugh. "i'm the soulless whorepig cunt here."

i grab my leather biker jacket an leave the club before i end up glassing the ugly bastard an i'm already round the corner heading back towards my Hill Street gaff before Amy catches up w/me an i don't even hear her runnin up behind me, i just hear "right, you fuckin bastard!" an i turn just in time to get twatted round the side a the head. i try to walk away but she continues the attack w/a barrage of slaps an scratches at my face an she's screaming at me like a bitch so i punch her once an knock her on the floor right down in the gutter by the side a the road. people in the stream of passing cars gawping out the winnders like i'm sum sorta monsta, cept one kid who sticks his head out an yells, "slap her down, old son!" Amy gets up an starts running away back to the club, "right, you bastard," she spits, stabbing a finger at her arm, "i'm gonna go an do 3 grams a whizz straight in my arm an then i'm gonna fuck his brains out so think about that when you're lyin in bed on your own tonight."

"have a lovely evening," i tell her as i calmly turn an walk away, secretly seething inside.

"you're an asshole!" she screams.

"yeah, well..." i shrug. "you're an asshole = you outmanouvered me. that's all that means."

"i'll have you fuckin *ass-raped*!" she screeches like sum evil wraith. an she screams the words w/such venom like she's wretched them up from the pit of her stomach.

\* \* \*

early morning. it's a beautiful silver sky. the city is smothered in a swirling damp, white mist an the Autumn sun like a pale disc that ain't chuckin out any heat at all is just coming up behind the Rotunda building. the peculiar silence of the street. an in the mist like a scene from a Jack the Ripper film or sum thing i hear stiletto heels striking the pavement. i know those footsteps. they're sharp angry footsteps, like distant gunshots an i know they're heading this way. an then the brick comes smashing throo my winnder. it's like 5 a.m or sum where abouts an i've not really been to bed, i been up lyin on the sofa listenin to Hawkwind albums most a the night. the brick lands on the floor in a shower a glass an a course i know who the fuck it is so i don't even flinch i just calmly go over to the winnder an sure as shit it's Amy down there, her hair is all fucked up an her make-up's run all over her face, an i smile out the broken winnder an shout down: "well, i see your little honeymoon didn't last long. loverboy's fucked you off then has he?"

they've been doing sum kinda roadworks down there an they got a little hole dug w/these orange barriers round it an Amy finds another big rock in the mound a dirt they've left on the pavement, she stands there impishly w/it poised above her head ready to throw an goes: "you gonna let me up or what?" an i tell her course i'm not gonna let her in she just threw a fuckin brick throo my fuckin winnder. an then i wave her down w/my hand an tell her to cool it down, pointing down the road where a police patrol car is lurking but she stands scowling up at me an launches the rock anyway but this time it misses the winnder an bounces off the wall. "oh just fuckin great," i tell her, "that's it, bring the blue-bottles round my gaff why don't you?" the cop car speeds up, flicking on its blue lights an skids to a halt right by Amy an the 2 blue-bottles get out all purposeful an one of them grabs her by the arm an yells, "what you think you're doing?"

i peer down an indicate to the cop the broken winnder, down at Amy, an then back to the winnder again w/a shrug of resignation. Amy says sum thing to the cop that i can't hear an the cop shouts up at me, "you gonna let her in? i'd like to get her off the street."

"no i'm not gonna let her in," i shout back.

"You're not going to let her in? she told me she lives here."

"no, i'm not. she's a stone-faced liar, she don't live here."

"you're not going to let her in at all? not at any point? is that what you're saying?" the cop still has hold of Amy by the arm.

"i'd rather go scuba-diving down the sewers of Calcutta." i laugh.

"so," the cop holds out his palms but he don't laugh one bit like cops never do, "what do you want us to do then, sir?"

an then Amy starts thrashin about, screamin from the pit of her stomach again, musterin up an anguished flood a crocodile tears: "YOU WANNA KNOW WHAT HAPPENED? YOU REALLY WANNA KNOW WHAT HAPPENED? HE RAPED ME, OK! HE RAPED ME. HE RAPED ME. HE RAPED ME!"

i just look down an tell her quietly an calmly, "everyone disregards your bullshit, Amy. everyone knows you're fuckin crazy."

the cop car's flashing blue lights pick out beer bottle empties, paper cups, an assortment of other debris strewn all over the street.

i ask the cop if he can't just get rid of her, take her away? an the cop says yeah he can do that an he pushes Amy an tells her to walk away now, to go home, or find sum where else to stay. but she bites his hand an holds on like a bulldog an then the 2 cops wrestle her to the floor an cuff her up. she's kicking an screaming like a banshee as they throw her in the back a the squad car an she looks up at me an screams, her eyes full a those pretend tears: "go to your dictionary an look up 'mitigating circumstances' you stupid fuckin bastard." an then the blue bottles slam the door on our law expert an cart her away.

man, i tell you, that girl got more moves than a Chinese abacus. they'll probably end up driving her to a darkened back street sum place where she'll let the pair of them slip it to her long dick style before lettin her go free. she always wangles herself out of it, man. somehow she always manages to wangle out of it.

until i can sort out a glazier i botch up a makeshift repair on the winnder w/cardboard an sticky tape. i take off my Nirvana tshirt an then finally i roll onto the bed. my alone-ness is whole an complete an all-encompassing. never had anyone to share anything with, an never wanted no one either, even if i've always been searching for sum thing i'll never find i can at least say i never needed nuthin from no one. regardless of anything i'm right where i want to be, just sum skinny kid drifting throo life like a paper cup blowin down the street in the wind, sum dark abstract shape all alone in the world w/at least a real comprehension of the vast scale of distance between me an the rest of the human race.

    you can resign yourself to lonliness but in the end find sanctuary in it. it's like the infinite dark space between galaxies. an now i just lie here in sum kinda opiatic tranquility, an the cool mornin air comin throo the broken winnder pane feels beautiful on my skin an i feel like i can sit an stare into dislocated nothingness, return to the black womb a death like i been lobotomised w/no feelings of either love nor hate an just this feelin a freedom from envy / freedom from pain. clock on the wall has stopped ticking. but there's no such thing as time anyway, only in the degradation of our cells, our structure breaking down bit by bit. that's the only kind a time you need to know. you need to know when you're old an you need to know when it's all over. until then you live the life you wanna live the way you wanna live it.

    fuck it, i pour a whisky an spark up a spliff an shove an American porno tape in the VHS player. there's a few seconds a screen static an then it clears to a brunette wearing just her underwear sitting on the sofa in her living room. there's a knock at the door an she answers. it's sum dago-wop delivery guy in red baseball cap an he says: "hello, lady. did you order pizza?" an he smiles an pulls his pizza-boy apron aside to reveal his cock hanging out his pants an adds: "w/mucho extra Italian sausage...?" the bird goes, "sure did, but gee i don't have any extra for a tip." so she lets him in her gaff an gets on her knees an sucks him off instead an in the end he pulls out her mouth an cums all over the pizza before making her eat it.

it wasn't revealed in the storyline whether the pizza was cooked to a high standard or not but i imagine it must a gone cold anyway cuz it took the wop an aeon to shoot his bolt. but she laps the pizza up all the same an at least pretends to enjoy it going, "mmm mmm oh yeah, daddy."

# 6

there's no air conditioning in the place so when Rob an Danny the 2 doormen swing the doors open the blast of heat from the packed basement bar hits you as you walk in. Danny already clocks us as we approach the place an he goes, "well, well, well, if it ain't the Birmingham City All Stars." an i don't know why he chooses me cuz i ain't carryin but he cops hold a my arm as i attempt to slip past him an he says w/a smile, "what narcs we got on us then, sunshine?" an he starts goin throo my pockets an when he don't find nuthin he don't even bother checkin out Superfast or Electric... who's the one w/the gear. outta curiosity i am compelled to ask him, "so why you searchin me?" an Danny just winks an says: "reputation goes before you, kiddo."

i mean fuckin hell, why me? you only gotta take one look at Superfast to know he's already hepped up on the Phennies or sum thing, his lidded eyes are gone, man.

DJ in this joint calls himself DJ Purgatory. last time i was here was to see a local rock band called Fayre Warning play, that musta been '87 or sum time. but now it's September 10th 1991, an i'm in the Ingram Lounge on Dalton Way before we head up to Goldwyn's for the Nine Inch Nails gig. the joint ain't no lounge at all. the Ingram is another subterranean dive-bar w/inadequate plumbing. it's humid in here like it's got its own tropical eco-system or sum thing an the warm dank carpet sticks to your feet. we're all pretty amped-out an we need a kick so after we get our drinks we head straight for the miniscule gents toilets to do sum Bazooka but tonight the plumbing's fucked again an it's ankle deep in overflowing piss so we go into the marginally drier women's cubicles that under the circumstances serve as a unisex affair an it's chock full so we have to join the queue. from back in the club you can hear DJ Pugatory's gruff cigarettes-an-Jack Daniel's voice introducing Black Sabbath before *Iron Man* comes pile-driving throo the walls.

i never in my life ever knew another

sleazeball like Electric. greased back thinning hair an mustache, always wears the gaudiest Hawaiian shirts an tonight he's got these cheap gold avaitor sunglasses on that he's obviously picked up in a one-quid store an he looks like sum kind a minature version of Ron Jeremy gone awry. for a while now he's bin tryin to sell this candle, man. he's never got it w/him, he keeps it in a glass display case at home an he claims it's only 1 of 3 left in the world. he claims it's made by the Nazis out of exterminated Jew fat. more than likely Electric just bought the fucking thing from dodgy Dave's market stall or sum where an embossed a Swastika an a fake number in it but sum how he's got this official looking Nazi-stamped paperwork endorsing it from the Westerbork death camp. but that ain't exactly impossible to fake an the dweeb's also got a full chickenshit sales pitch he gives people. "there's kind of a dull smell to it, you know?" Electric says, "an if you were to light it you'd get that burning flesh smell as if you were cooking salty bacon." probably all such bullshit. but so far everyone in the Ingram Lounge he's tried pitching it to is like Jesus Christ nah nah, why would i wanna buy sumthin like that? but it's a sick city, man, an you can bet your life sooner or later sum lousy fucker will hand over cash for the deplorable thing but in this joint i'm surprised no one has belted him one yet. Electric is a vile defective creature tho an when he laughs its like the pained cry of a crow, like an awful screeching eeeaghh eeeagh eeeagh.

in the girls' cubicle the 3 of us drink our drinks an smoke the coke/acapulco gold cocktail we've got on the go. "you know, you're in the wrong manor," Superfast advises Electric. "you wanna sell it at a Skrewdriver gig or sumthin. they'd love that shit, it'd sell like a hot cake."

Electric takes a long toke on the blunt an says thoughtfully: "yeah, you know Hilter did so much good for Germany an Europe i'm just shocked that we British wanted to kill him."

"how you work that out?" Superfast asks.

"well, if he hadn't dominated the Jews like he did, wiped so many of them out, Germany could well now be a Jewish majority country. They'd be in the driving seat of Europe. Fact is if you don't dominate sum one, they'll dominate you. it's horrible really, but it's set in human nature, innit?"

"you think," Superfast goes, "the Jews woulda dominated Germany?"

"for fuckin sure. an eventually the whole a Europe, too. look what they done to the Palestinians. cept they'd a settled in Germany instead, claimed that land as the New Jerusalem instead of Israel." he flicks ash from the enda the joint down the toilet pan an flushes it. "fuckin obvious. they ain't bothered about no mass a land they can call home. *Israel* is in the

Zionist heart, it's political. not geographical."

i snatch the blunt outta Electric's fingers an say: "never mind all that shit. it's my turn, gimme a toke on that." Electric lets go of the blunt an continues vehemently, "you know, calling yourselves the chosen race an then artificially creating a whole religious ideology around it to support the proposition is fundamentally no different to calling yourselves the master race an creating a whole political philosophy to support that. 360 degrees an zero is the same point."

i just toke on the blunt, man. i try not to think about all this shit. i don't even know how accurate his dissertation is. in my view socialism is a nice idea, its heart is in the right place but the ongoing behaviour of the human race constantly indicates that reality just don't work that way. we might evolve past it all but it ain't ever happened yet so it don't matter what anyone duz or anyone sez, cuz the meaning behind it don't ever change. society's all whacked out, messed up. people ain't gettin their voices heard an people are so narcissistic when they don't get their voices heard they get violent. it's always the same, only the faces are different w/each new generation.

it's sort of amazing really cuz Electric got these weird childlike glittering eyes that peer right into you all naïve an enquiring an shining in innocence like he really just don't understand the stuff he comes out with an i dunno what his family background is but i'm guessing he's never truly experienced love an it's hardened him to the point he just ain't got no empathy for anybody else an people hardened in such a manner get sucked into little groups like all this neo Nazi shit he's got into an them sortsa people havta find a way to inflict their inner pain on sum body else. but socialists do that as well, project their inner hatred onto the nation. they hate themselves so they hate the sea an the ship their sailing in.

then amidst the chattering voices queueing for the toilets there's a sudden jarring loud copknock on the cubicle door an it's Danny the doorman again, who by the way looks like Philthy Animal Taylor outta Motorhead cept he got this terrible 1983 mullet haircut, an he tells us we gotta leave right now. "you're stinkin the place out w/that shit, fellas," he goes, waving his hand before his face. "what the fuck you got in that thing?" he says as he escorts us all off the premises. an i tell him, man. i tell him it's a touch a the old Bazooka an so Danny tells us to get the fuck out w/our Bazooka then an not come back no more w/that shit again.

we head out across the market place an as we walk throo the skeletal empty market stalls a dosed up Superfast is doin this shit attempt at shadow boxing, throwing straights out in front of him an mixin it up w/what i think are sposed to be karate kicks an he's spittin out his words, goin: "...mess w/me, man. i'll knock his stupid fuckin mullet right off his fuckin head!"

cuttin throo Martineau Place we're confronted by sum smiling fucking mongoloid pillock giving out Jesus flyers for the big Pentecostal church in Hockley. "you know a man called Jesus Christ?" he yells after us as we walk on past him. an i go, "nah, i never heard a no Jesus an Christ. are they comedians? i heard a Laurel an Hardy." the Jesus freak comes up behind me an puts his hand on my head an tries to chant sum twaddle of a prayer for me like he's tryna excorcise the demons he thinks are livin inside me or sum shit like that but i knock his hand away an tell him, "fuck off, you ginger-headed melon" an the Jesus freak pulls a sad face an sez, "Jesus loves you, my brother." till this mutant had Jesus he had heroin. an you can still see it in his face a mile off. he's got those indolent dead heroin eyes staring out his skull like 2 dull stones. sooner or later he'll be back on it.

it's like about a week after the Handsworth riots now, walking cross town there's still an imposing police presence, sum of them carrying guns, an all over the city black folk are still looking edgy, nervous. no doubt shit-scared a police van full of SPG might screech to a halt any moment an all jump out an baton the living fuck outta them. you can see the edginess in their darting eyes.

one day man will have the scope to spread out across the infinite universe. but until we have the technolgical means to do so, we will remain like rats in a cage, over-populated, turning on each other.

my ears are ringing after the NIN gig, where i sold sum stupid 17 year old kid draggin sum skanky punk bird around w/him looking for drugs a Zube cough lozenge for 5 quid. we end up at sum kebab/burger joint up the Soho Road, it's like 2 a.m or sum thing now an there's sum blubbery skinhead lying on the floor between the tables who's been gutted like a trout, his flabby wet mouth gaping open.

all i remember about the gig was NIN doing *Head Like a Hole* an every body down in the mosh pit goin wild, stage diving an sending bottles a beer fizzing throo the air to the sound of heavy synthesized bass lines an overdriven guitars fed throo distortion peddles. there was things goin on like amps blowin up in showers a sparks as drinks got sprayed over electronic circuitry. fuckin wild.

the Soho Road is chock full a prozzies but they're not the kind a prozzies i'd stump up any dosh for. the fat skinhead kid's sprawled out unconscious an looking at the massive patch a blud staining his white tshirt it looks like he got it in the liver an to my eyes he's turnin an awful jaundiced colour, kid don't look very well at all an i'm seriously thinking he might not survive.

place is pretty full but as usual in these situations nobody saw nuthin an everyone just carries on eating their burgers an kebabs while this skinhead is dyin on the ground an there's a policeman kneeling down pressing a bunched up towel on the wound tryin to stem the flow a blud that's spilling out onto the tiled floor until the meat wagon arrives.

as far as the Turkish kebab guy is concerned it all seems to be business as usual so we get our burgers an make our way to a table near the winnder. Electric does sum dumb shit thing like leaning over an pretending he's gonna dip one of his fries in the pool a blud on the floor laughing hysterically an the cop points his finger, looks at us an makes sum incomprehensible stern command but i'm so utterly spackered on whisky an the white blizzard coursing throo my veins an in addition we dropped these microdots an we all keep having these fits of laughter that just won't stop. i don't properly know what the fuck is goin on but the cop's pressin this towel on the wound tryna stop the flow a blud an he points a finger at the dying skinhead an goes, "settle down! settle down! this is very serious. this lad's bin *knifed!*" an i try to restrain myself but i can't an i go, "that's sum brilliant detective work, officer."

an a course it ain't what you say it's the way that you say it an i don't think he at all liked the way i said it. the cop gives me the old stinkeye like he thinks we're just a bunch a delinquent scumbags an says sumthin along the lines of: i know what the deal w/you little dipshits is so think yourselves lucky i've got this to see to tonight, now fuck off home. but we don't take too much notice, an although we don't say anythin else we just sit there an finish our burgers.

we're hangin about on the corner beneath a murky street light lookin for sum where to get another drink but all the pubs are closed now an there's nuthin else to do so we're about to flag a black cab down an shoot off home when this little greasy-haired strutting dwarf comes striding up who sez his name is Big Dave. an it's like a really bizarre situation becuz he just comes from out a nowhere like he's materialised out another dimension. he's got these red raw scabs on his bulbous forehead. Big Dave shakes our hands amiably, like sum kinda door-to-door double-glazin salesman an tells us to call him Big D. he's like 3 an a half foot tall but about the same in width an he's dressed in nuthin but a grey hooded sweatshirt an a pair a massive khaki cargo shorts that come down to sumthin stupid like 2 inches above his ankles on which he's wearin Bugs

Bunny socks.

"hey," Big D goes. "so you guys lookin for another drink, yeh? yeh?" an we're like yeah we are. so this little dwarf spins sum yarn about this friend of his who got a liquor store round the corner an he can get us some take-outs if we let him have just one can a beer.

"what you after?" Big D asks.

Superfast shrugs an sez, "anythin... i dunno... 6 cans a Carling."

"yeh yeh, give us a tenner an i'll fetch em for yer." Big D holds out his hand an sez: "you just wait here, i'll be like 5 minutes, yeh yeh."

Electric an me watch all incredulous as Superfast just goes an gives him a tenner an Big D marches off prenty pronto  like a little wind-up soldier an turns the corner on his heel.

"you stupid fucker," Electric goes, kicking a stone angrily. "he ain't gonna come back, you shit for brains."

so we walk to the corner an look down the street an the dwarf has vanished. no sign of him an no sign a no drinks shop either. "i just don't fuckin believe *you*" Electric sez, waving his hands about. "what a fucking dolt."

we're all still pretty buzzin an Superfast gets the idea of headin over to Walsall cuz there's a drinkin place on Station Street called the Super Star. it's owned by this Yardie who calls himself Bad Juju an his group a Yardie cronies an you can get a drink anytime a night till like 5am. Bad Juju is like sum Mr. Bigstuff in his community. his bar is just an entrance w/this little prison-door slider thing that they look outta to see who you are before they let you in. no sign on the wall outside or nuthin. they got no drinks licence or anythin, you'll never find the joint if you don't already know about it an you only know about it if sum black guy took you down there sum time. it is, as it were, by invitation only an you can skin up in there no problem. they got no drinks on tap or no spirits either, the serving counter is just a line a decorator's paste tables an it's just cans a Redstripe out the fridge. the only thing i don't like bout the joint is the music cuz it's all Reggae stuff that i just never been into at all. but it's alright, as long as i gotta drink i can endure it. i got this friend Columbian Gary who took me down there 1 time an Superfast reckons i can get us in so i say to him, i say: sure, yeah, it's worth a shot.

Superfast remains deadly quiet in the taxi, sitting with his arms folded, staring down at his Vans an Electric just keeps repeating "you stupid fucker" over an over. there's a pause for like only 10 seconds then again he shakes his head an goes, "Jesus Christ... you stupid fucker."

"shut up now, Electric," i say. "it's not even *your* tenner is it?"

"you gotta admit he's a stupid fucker," Electric sez.

"alright, alright, yeah," i concede. "it was a stupid thing to do. but just leave it now."
we travel not talkin for a good while an then as the taxi trundles past the Perry Barr dogs Superfast shifts uncomfortably in his seat, shakes his head an goes, "i can't believe i just did that."

"yeah, *beeeecuzzz* you're a stupid fucker," Electric sez, prodding him with his finger. "Jesus H Christ, man. think about it... you got *stiffed* by a fuckin.... *dwarf!*"

Superfast goes, "you know, i could just punch you in the face right now" an Electric responds like, "yeah? well why don't you?" then they start fighting in the back a the taxi, the taxi driver hits the brakes an pulls over near the Park Hall housing estate an demands 15 quid an then orders us all out onto the street right there where we're still like about 3 miles from where we're heading.

musta been like 3.30 a.m when we walked up outside the Super Star an then the bastards wunt let us in an we weren't about to argue becuz this big fuckin Yardie type w/one eye an a big fuckin scar across his face comes out an he's like 6ft 8 w/dreds down to his waist an he sez if we don't fuck off he's gonna break our legs. we poke around a little way up the street for a while an we all drop a couple a microdots to keep us topped up but the night has totally turned to rust so we have to go huntin for another taxi back home an we decide we better look for a different firm becuz the last one bound to have gotten on the blower an told all his cohorts not to pick this bunch a bozos up.

we wander round onto Park Street making our way to the taxi-rank an parked up in a hotdog van is this dimwitted guy we know who calls himself Ace. Ace has got these stupefied boggle eyes an blonde curly hair that makes him look like Harpo out the Marx bros. he's like a little slow or sum thing. he's definitely not firing on all cylinders but he's like just this little pipsqueek shitstain who sumhow figured out how to make a ton a money. in any case, Ace is parked up in this hotdog van, it's all painted up nice an professional but he's called the fuckin thing The Sausage Jockey. liveried in big fuckin red letters in the form a hotdog sausages, drippin in splodges a yellow mustard right down the side a the van: **THE SAUSAGE JOCKEY**.

so we can't help ourselves but go over there to taunt him an Ace gets out his seat an slides the service winnder open an goes, "aright, lads. what i get you?" an i go, "hey, Aceface, nice van. you actually know what a sausage jockey is?" Ace's boggle eyes roll around witlessly in their sockets an i remember how we used to call him Satallite becuz when you ask him a question it takes him ages to answer like he's waitin for the signal to beam back down to his brain. he sez, "fast food innit? like, you know, hotdogs... but served as fast as a racehorse."

i don't even bother enlightening him. "whatever you say, Aceface. hey, you sell like... them cones of hot buttered sprouts?"

Ace looks at me all perplexed, shakes his head sluggishly like he's punch-drunk an goes, "nah, i never heard a no food place ever serving sumthin like hot buttered sprouts."
we all stagger off, falling about, laughing. "hot buttered sprouts," Superfast sez. "oh man, that's your best one in ages, you cunt."

we stagger over the pelican crossing an i stop an have a piss up the Sister Dora statue, our laughter echoing around the buildings.

the microdots are kickin in so we're all shot to pieces an all the way home in the back a the fragrant, perfume-scrubbed black-cab we're repeating "hot buttered sprouts" at regular intervals an every single time one of us says it we all degenerate into fits of rabid laughter until we're struggling to breathe. the Pakistani taxi driver is laughing as well, but he don't even know what he's laughin at, he's just laughin at us. must a bin thinkin we're a right bunch a white twats.

# 7

here's a thing. i'm drinking in this bar that i don't know the name of overlooking the canal down where Granville Street meets Gas Street. an she don't spot me in my vantage point behind a pillar but down by the canal near where a bunch a narrowboats are moored i see Amy arguing w/sum other poor bastard an he's like sum simpering idiot who's all effeminate cuz he looks like the lead singer of Scritti Politti. an out the winnder i watch Amy screaming an waving her arms about as the Scritti Politti kid minces about all impassive an lookin down at his patent leather shoes an i smile as Amy launches herself at him with a wild, deranged flying kick to his groin an the dweeb doubles over an lies there unmoving on the ground as she strides away laughing like the maniac that she is.

i'm heading over to XLs rock club just off 5 Ways. i'm short a cash so i was planning to sell a shit load of E's. i disguise the E's by decanting a tin a mints into the trashcan an replacing them. there's like 200 E's in the tin that i plan to flog for a tenner a pop. the price is really only a fiver an my cut is whatever i choose to get for them over that. but i get to the door an the doorman pulls me aside just as i try to slip in. he's wearing a lapel badge that sez his name is Mike. Mike goes throo my pockets an pulls out the tin. "what we got here then, whiteboi?" he goes popping open the hinged lid an looking inside. "mints aren't they Sherlock," i go, holding out my hand for him to hand them back. "think i was born yesterday," he says shaking his head. "these things ain't no mints like i evva seen, boi."

"you gonna give me em back?" i say. "they're not really mine an you don't wanna mess w/the guy who they belong to."

"well, i tell you what," the big black bastard smiles condescendingly, putting the tin in the inside pocket of his black bomber jacket, "come an see me when you leave an i'll give em you back then."

"alright," i warn him, "but listen, Mikey, i'm really not kiddin around. see my friend who they belong to, he's got this bad breath, i mean it really stinks, man, an he likes to freshen it up. he really likes those mints, see this guy eats a lot a Chinese curry, you might even know him.... get my drift?"

"oh yeah? whaddya gonna do, you liddle fuckin scrag-end?" he cuts me off. "who ya think ya fuckin with?"

i try to give him one last chance an tell him dead straight, "look, man, those mints belong to Slant Eye Joe."

this goon wants everyone to think he's sum kind a big shot, thinks he's hot shit but he's forgettin he works nightclub doors an the Tag

Heuer on his wrist is a blatant fake an his shoes are scuffed an his bulging suit ain't cut from no Savile Row cloth it's from Suits-U or sum cheapo joint. he's a cunt. he's Mr. Cunt of Cunt Street, Cunt Town, Cunt Country. just a nobody from a long ancestral line of nofuckinbodies.

"Slant Eye who?" he says, mockingly.

"Joe... Slant Eye Joe."

"Ohhhh right, Slant Eye Joe, eh?" he says. an Mike the bouncer's really on a roll now, feeling his feet, he bends over an laughs, flashing his big white teeth an slaps his backside an his head wobbles from side to side as he thinks of every racial slur he can: "Well, you tell this ping-pong, pan face chinksta, whoever he is, that he can come on down here himself an kiss my big black booty."

realising this low I.Q buffoon don't understand the weight of the situation i look at the floor an run my hand throo my hair an i shoot him sum kind a bemused expression but this goon just ain't ever gettin it, he's well up on his own ego trip. "oh shit," i warn him. "you've just gone way past your station, Crackerjack."

but he ain't interested an at this point 2 a the other big goons come over eyeballing me an i'm thinkin oh here we fuckin go again an the 3 of them man-handle me out the front door an throw me on the pavement outside. they slam the door shut an i hear the bolt go across from inside an then i hear 3 big silverbacks laughin like drunken gypsies but they'll be laughin on the other side a their faces after i've spoken to Slant Eye. they ain't got a clue cuz they're empty inside. it's like watching actors on the teevee, they got a way of makin you think they feel sum thing but really it's all just an image, an act. an it's all really the same in reality.

i'm kicking a Pepsi can along as i walk home. so it don't matter what anyone duz or anyone sez cuz the meaning is always the same, an the meaning is nothingness, a void, oblivion. the only thing people feel an the only thing anyone understands is getting fuckin coldcocked. people only understand pain. the whole a humanity is locked into sum kind a self-destruction an there's nuthin any of us can do about it, we're heading for sumthin catastrophic like we're programmed to self destruct an no sequences in the process can be changed.

after a bit i stamp the can totally flat an kick it into the gutter.

* * *

this morning before leaving the gaff i watched this old porn film from the early 70s on VHS called Garage Girls that was about a bunch a girl mechanics that opened their own repair shop an fucked all the customers who came in to get their cars fixed.

i'm not certain if the work on the vehicles

themselves was carried out to a proper mechanical standard, the director of this film didn't see fit to make that clear, unless of course i am misunderstanding sum thing. but i mean, would you even complain? i'm talking about if you'd just fucked this girl over the hood an then cum between her tits but then your car fucks up again not even 5 miles down the road. you'd probably let the issue slide, so it seems to me these rip off little skanks could be gettin away w/murder. 'course, it's just sum cheap-shot porno film, i know that. i just can't help wondering about these things an applying them to reality.

walking along Curzon Street i ran into this kid i know called Disco Dave. he's this club kid who's like 27 years old or sumthin an he's comin down the street drinkin a can a Tizer, lookin like he just had electro-shock treatment with this dyed silver hair all sticking out at the sides like pigeon wings. he's wearing a red velour suit an silver boots an these big bug-eye sunglasses. Disco's like one a the cool kids, you know, an everybody kinda hangs on his every move just cuz a the way he dresses, like he's just walked straight outta *Granny Takes A Trip* up the Kings Road down London. but he gets his clobber from same gaffs as me, like *The Razor's Edge* an *Vagabond's* an *72 Hurst Street*, he just buys different stuff to me. i asked him if he's cruising for a little sumthin an he told me no way, man. he don't drink or take nuthin no more, he's cleanin his act up. Disco claimed he's taken up a bit a cycling, yeah yeah, gettin fit an all that. he was bouncing on his heels. hyped up on health, he sed. never felt better. he didn't look much different to me but you gotta understand this kid ain't firing on all cylinders an he lives on a different planet, man. i punched him on the arm all the same an sed, "yeah, that's fantastic, Disco. do it, man."

course, you absolutely know he's fulla shit. truth is i've heard him say all this before. the bullshittin bastard's just out a dosh cuz he's squandered it all on drink, that's all. he's an alright kid though, i like Disco. in small doses.

\* \* \*

i'm lyin in bed, it's like 3 a.m an i'm stirred by a sudden high-pitched beep beep beep beep from outside an the flat is strobed w/flashing blue light. i go to the winnder an see a meat wagon reversing up outside. the 2 ambulance crew get out an open the back doors an Amy comes stumbling out the back an i'm just staring open mouthed thinkin what the fuck is goin on here. so i go down in the street wearing only my Levi's, there's a light flurry of snow an i'm shivering an i'm like "what's goin on?" Amy's make-up is a mess again an her hair is like a fucking bird's nest, she's wearing one stiletto shoe an clutching the other one, heel broken off, in her hand an she's wearing a tiny white dress that's now filthy an Jesus Christ she just looks like sum half-emaciated dime-store crack-whore out here. she can't walk an the ambulancewoman who's looking well pissed off is holding her up. Amy is barely intelligible an she smiles this big stupid ianane smile at me an says "hello, Mark, darling." an though nuthin should really surprise me w/this skank ass chick i'm just incredulous, going like what the holy fuck is goin on? the ambulanceman says: "well, she's certainly drunk, i'll tell you that for nuthin."

"yeah yeah, i can see she's drunk," i can't help but let out a laugh. "what's she doing here?"

"she told us she lives here."

"well, she don't. she don't live here at all," i say.

"sum body found her unconscious lying in the middle of Corporation Street an called us. we had to bring her cuz if we'd left her where she was sum thing nasty might have happened to her, know what i mean?"

Amy eyeballs the geezer an goes, "i haven't dun anythin, you're not arresting me, you bald-headed prick!"

"i'm not even a copper," he tells her, laughing. "i'm a paramedic."

"alright," i concede, "give her to me, i'll take

her in."

so i get a hold of her round the waist an steer her towards my front door an the ambulance crew jump back in the meat wagon an the thing lumbers away.

after getting Amy up the stairs an into the flat i try to stand her up but she bounces off the sideboard, staggers across the room an crashes over the coffee table an ends up wedged between the table an the sofa, giggling. she don't understand a word i try an say to her. i pick her up an throw her on the sofa an i go back to bed. after about half an hour she crawls into bed next to me an starts kissing me. "you know i love you," she slurs. "don't you want to fuck me, Mark?" an she pulls off her dress an spreads her legs an says dreamily, "i'll just lie here an let you fuck me. god, i want you to fuck me really hard, i want you to punish me for being so bad to you all the time." she's breathing heavily, writhing an pressing herself against me an she's holding my cock in her hand. "an when you're gonna come i want you to pull out an come in my mouth. i want you to come right in my mouth, right in my mouth. will you come in my mouth, Mark? i'll just lie here an let you come in my mouth, an i'm gonna take it all cuz i want you to punish me."

\* \* \*

i'm woken up at 8 a.m by the noize of Electric's motorbike outside. Amy's totally amped out comatose an just to top it all off, she's pissed the bed. she looks so pale an delicate lying there naked. an she is. she really is. she is delicate an vulnerable an even though she deserves to be kicked to the curb most a the time you know that really she's just like a child an sum times it's hard to be cruel back to her an she's got the little scars on her arms where she's cut herself an you always want to wrap her up an protect her. she's lost an broken just like the rest of us an it has to bleed out of her cuz she can't bury it inside herself like most people can an it don't even help if you tell her you understand cuz she don't think nobody does. she just don't think nobody understands.

    but it's like this: as narrow an provincial as they are, people's interpretation of you will be filtered throo their own limited perceptions an translated into sumthin they can understand. an that's why no one truly understands anyone else an we are all ultimately alone in this world. sum times you just have to accept people are how they are for reasosns you will never comprehend, like watching actors on a teevee screen an they got this way of making you think they're feelin sum thing in relation to what they're sayin but really they're just a blank canvas onto which you're projecting your own emotions an they themselves don't feel nuthin. it's kind a like this internal purgatory we all exist in.

you look back an it's just like lookin at a roll a film stills. images of your life an you can remember the images but not the emotions or your thought processes. we were somewhere, i don't remember where, some bar or party. but i remember watching Amy this one time. she was smoking a cigarette. an she sat there watching teevee, smoking this cigarette, an i watched her just suddenly press the burning end into the back of her hand. she didn't even cry in pain or show any reaction like she didn't even know she was doing it, she just didn't even smell or feel her own flesh burn like her senses was numb to everything.

it's Sunday an i heard the approaching clatter of Electric's clapped out 1975 Benelli Tornado 650-S from like a mile away. a supercool motorbike for any body else but Electric's let his go to rot an he pulls up outside in a cloud a stinking black smoke an leaves the thing still smoldering on the pavement outside an he comes up the flat an he's askin me for sum fuckin cola an i'm just in fuckin shock at his audacity, going "now how the fuck a man like you gonna raise adequate funds for coke, man?" Electric smiles a great big crooked-tooth smile an rubs his fingertips together an says:

"ohh, don't you worry, sunshine, i got the lettuce, bruv. yeah yeah yeah, i got the lettuce." an i mean he's all fuckin buzzin, happy as a lark.

"how the fuck?" i go.

"i sold the Jewfat candle." he looks fantastically pleased.

an i'm absolutely incredulous that sum one, anyone, ever bought that gruesome shit an Electric adds gleefully, "yeah yeah, to this neo Nazi skinhead over in Bloxwich."

an i dunno what else to think an i dunno what to say, i just look at Electric blankly an go: "have i ever told you you've never done anything other than make my flesh crawl?" an i just gotta ask, "look, man, was that candle really what you sed it was?" an Electric glances at me sideways flitting his beady eyes w/their spectral dark rings round them but he won't properly look me in the face an sez, "yeah course it woz." but i dunno what to make of it cuz this kid's always on sum chickenshit bullcrap trip. it really is probably a load a shit. an i hope it is, i hope it is cuz that kinda thing really freezes the blud in my veins.

but in any case, i flog him the wrap a basuco for 50 quid anyway an he stuffs it down his sock. basuco's like the low-grade stuff, mixed w/touch a the old coca paste or Christ only knows what else, cheapest shit on the streets a Colombia, undoubtably imbibed by crack-whores an their pimps but Electric just won't know the difference at all. an i don't even know why he bothers anyway, the effects of cheap speed last for hours, the rush induced by sum a the best cola lasts like 20 minutes, even tho while it lasts you definitely know you been chemically induced but it just don't last long enough at all. for real. but still, it just ain't worth the dosh you pay as i see things.

Electric's brought a couple a bottles a cheapo alley juice in his back-pack. he laughs becuz he thinks i'm joking when i say he makes my flesh crawl even though i'm not an he holds up the bottles an sez, "bring it on. dunno about you but i'm lookin forward to my next coma." an he flops down on the sofa as i also fetch out the Frogs - blotter acid, to be exact, Purple Ohms – for us to swill down w/the cheap booze.

like she's got sum kinda in-built radar for this stuff Amy is roused from her drunk-coma an rolls out the piss-stained bed. she picks up her handbag an heads straight for the bathroom where first you can hear her shower an then you hear her snorting sum thing an when she comes out it's like she's totally rejuvinated an despite the fact she's a fuck-up she's glowing w/youth an she looks like the reincarnation of Rita Hayworth an i never get how she manages it, just the luck of youth i suppose, i mean she's only like 22 but surely to Christ it can't last an she'll be a totally fucked-up hag by the time she's 30.

we bang the Frogs back w/the 2 bottles a Night Train Express that sum friend of Electric's bought him back from America that tastes like paint-stripper an by 11 a.m the 3 of us are in varying states of fucked-up, lying about the room staring at the walls flashed in the white glow comin from the teevee an Amy goes: "whew wee, this acid is powerful, man." an after the initial hit for how long i dunno but seemingly for hours i'm flat on my back w/the whole room going green/orange green/orange green/orange green/orange in my eyes an a hammering in my head that's like tonk tonk tonk tonk, like a hammer on a tin drum an i mean i don't need to tell no one - i'm totally fuckin skittled.

despite his Nazi sympathies Electric is this slightly fat, seemingly placid kid, rather cowardly in fact, like 23 years old or sum thing now an already balding w/this measly scrap of hair on his head an he don't get no women ever so i imagine he must be really pent up which is prob the reason for all of his frustrations w/the world around him. an i never got no idea how he keeps any weight on him at all cuz w/all the amphets Amy, me an Superfast are all like skinny to fuck speedfreaks. but it's like Electric is just this replica of a human being, so maudlin an spectral it's as if he's only human on the outside but there's just nuthin inside him that makes him 1 of us.

but i dunno, it's not that i believe in any kind a human soul. i don't an never have. in the final analysis life don't mean anything. people place far too much value on human life. in the end, it's all bullshit. on a universal scale, human beings w/all their art an literature an architecture an for all their splittin of atoms an putting men on the moon, observing diseases in laboratories, are pretty much meaningless. if the whole earth went pop like a balloon an disappeared right now it wouldn't make an iota of difference. the only thing that matters in the here an now is our own subjective universe.

truth is, this realm only exists beacuse we have a consciousness endowed w/the propensity for philosophical perception an the ability to quantify it throo sum form of expression. but you can't control any of it, we're all ensnared in a chaotic series of events that long predate our current circumstances. but i still believe in individuation. people need to become transpolitics. people need to realise politics is small thought an this world can neither be grasped nor expressed intellectually. therefore, it's not totally off the dial to say nuthin is really real an solid an whole beyond the impetus humans subjectively place on it. but people are too stupid, man. they're just too stupid to see throo these portals of realisation.

so you can say what you like. just leave

me to my drink an my drugs an the life i want to live. take it or leave it, don't matter to me what anyone thinks.

Amy's chucked on my Depeche Mode tshirt an she's sprawled spark out on the floor, legs splayed apart in just the tshirt an her knickers an you know, i mean she just don't give 2 fucks who's around an you can see her big nipples throo the tshirt an Electric keeps having this little shifty gawp, like staring right between her legs, giving her the eye of the rapist an i'm thinking it's probably best never to leave him alone w/her becuz he'd probably attempt the old *manoeuvre sur les derrière* on her but then i think what the fuck, man. even if she hadn't nodded off on sumthin akin to a g-ber daze she'd probably fuckin let him slip her one up the Gary Glitter anyway. it's seems to me like she pretty much lets any fucker give her one.

Amy's mother was in a car crash on the Aston Expressway bout 6 months ago, got her spinal cord fused, an they prescribed her Oxycodone to kill the pain an that stuff"s like 10 times more potent than morphine or sum thing insane like that an i mean as good as anythin you can get on the street an Amy steals the tablets out the medicine cabinet, she's worked out that if you crush a couple of them up an snort them the hit you get is super intense but thing is after the initial rush, it just knocks you the fuck out like you bin punched by George Foreman an now she's sprawled unconscious half on the sofa, half on the floor, legs spread apart, her pussy on show throo her flimsy knickers so though Christ knows why i even care i get up an throw a blanket over her. Electric just smiles an it sounds like a joke but i don't think it is when he stares right between her legs an screws up his awful grey skin face in sum kind of atrophied grimace an goes: "let's eat her pussy out, man."

i'm kneeling on the floor w/my elbows resting on the coffee table, my drink in front of me, staring at the teevee watching sum thing about this inventor geezer Trevor Baylis who's invented a wind-up radio an the teevee reporter says once it goes into mass production this thing gonna revolutionise 3rd world countries, i mean you wind this clockwork radio up an it works just like any other radio an all incredulous i go, "wow, a clockwork fuckin radio man."

Electric blows out his cheeks like he's totally unimpressed an he shakes his head an says, "well, if he really wanted to help 3rd world countries he'd a bin better inventing a clockwork abortion machine. there's just too many of em."

"you know, you really are a nasty bastard," i tell him as i switch off the teevee an go over an put the Rolling Stones *Let It Bleed* album on the turntable an i whack up the volume.

Electric stares at me vacuously w/his

beady chickenshit solemn eyes widening an changes the subject, "you look like you're havin a bad trip, son."

"i'm not... *son*," i inform him.

"but you look like you are," he persists. "just relax," he leans over an pats me on the shoulder.

"*i am* relaxed," i tell him. an i know he's about to go off on one of his bullshit things of trying to *give* everybody a bad trip.

"but you've got that look. the look of a bad trip."

"well, so do you."

"i'm not," he says. "i'm feelin beautiful, man."

"well stop spreadin the bad vibe then," i go, "otherwise we'll all be havin a bad one. anyway... don't you wish you ate grass?" i ask, tryin to change the subject.

"grass?" Electric goes, "you mean like... *eating* weed?"

"nah, you fucking faggot, i mean actually eating grass. i mean like grass grass, the green green grass of home."

"why you ask that? why the fuck i wanna eat grass?"

"it's like when you see cows grazing in a field, man. that just looks really chill."

Electric's eyes glaze over an he thinks about it an he flops back on the sofa then says, "oh yeah, eatin grass would be dead chill. or...

or... be a fish, man. you know," he glides his hand throo the air, "just hangin there in the warm tropical water an even if there's no such thing as peace in this world that's about as close to it as you'd ever get."

"you know you look so awfully bloated," i tell him.

"yeah?"

"yeah, bloated. puffy, you know? all puffed up, like a puffer fish."

"i ain't talkin about no puffer fish, man," Electric goes. "i mean like a... i dunno, a beautiful silver glitterin tropical fish or sumthin just gliding about in all this warm water... yeah, just floating."

"no, no," i say. "i mean now, for real. right now you're all puffed up. your skin's all red an puffy, man. you're havin a... *reaction* to sumthin."

"SHIT," Electric screams. he gets up an goes to the mirror on the wall. "you're right man, i'm all puffed up like a puffer fish! why am i so red?"

"no shit, i'm tellin you," i say. even his hair, man, what last strands of it he has stubbornly holding on to their own grim existence, he spikes it up an then i start laughing an the more i look at him the more he metamorphosises into a puffer fish an his face becomes a strange shade a bright orange an he got these spikes stickin out his scalp, his whole fat torpid body becomes invisible to me an all i can see is this puffer fish head floating about an suddenly i can't stop laughin at him an when he talks i don't hear nuthin at all, just his pursed lips are like going pooh pooh pooh pooh.

"stop laughing, shit-for-brains. this is serious, man," Electric says grimly, staring into the mirror. his eyes have gone like Marty Feldman, all bulging like they're popping out their sockets.

i'm just fuckin spaced an i can see pink ping-pong balls bubbling out the speakers to *You Got the Silver* like a bubble machine, fillin the room an hangin in the air, thousands of them bubbling out the speakers an just floatin in the air. an they grow in size until one by one they go pop pop pop pop an all disappear.

an then i watch Electric's head expand an his brain explode upwards, drippin from the ceiling like green jelly stalactites.

an i'm rolling around on the sofa laughing till my stomach hurts.

\* \* \*

later in the afternoon i put on my Kohl eyeliner an we drop another tab an hit the street. sum how the 3 of us wind up in sum back street restaurant up Curzon Street before we walk over to the Black Horse on the student campus. while we're waiting for our food order we sit listening an nodding impatiently as the waiter spends 10 fucking minutes givin us the spiel about why they named their new own-brand house wine after the Portuguese explorer Vasco da Gama. the label on the bottle the waiter is holding close to his chest has a portrait of a noble looking bearded man who i presume is indeed a rendering of Vasco da Gama himself.

"...so, you know..." the waiter extols, "he explored new frontiers an melded new tastes an new experiences an that's exactly where we like to think we're going with our wine. indeed, it has a rich, full-bodied fruit base, pleasantly assuaged by subtle overtones of black pepper an finally a mellow aftertaste of liquorice; which is a bold an daring reference to da Gama's travels in India an the east." he offers forth the bottle of red for us to see. "perhaps you'd like to sample it," he adds. "i feel certain you'd apprecia..."

"yeah, i'll try sum," Amy pipes up. she leans right into my ear an sez,"i wish he'd cut those revolting black hairs stickin out his nose."

the waiter yanks a corkscrew out the pocket of his red waistcoat, uncorks the bottle w/a flourish an pours her like a half a wine-glass. Amy snatches it up an bangs it back in one gulp. she smacks her lips together sarcastically an sez, "it's disgusting. like bloody vinegar. we'll leave it."

she looks pretty good tonight. she's put on a tight Levi's denim jacket, a pink tutu, stripey tights an pink, patent leather Dr. Martens an her hair's all wild, down to her waist.

poor bastard waiter looks totally deflated when i extend 3 fingers an say flatly, "…we'll have Jack Daniel's, sunshine."

from the description on the menu even though we weren't totally 100% sure exactly what it was Amy an me both held up sum small amount of self-respect an had this peri peri chicken dish w/crispy potatoes called sumthin or other, sum pretentious name. but Electric asked the waiter for nuthin but a plate a peas. now i ask you, what kind a mutant goes into a mediterranean restaurant an orders just a plate a peas an gravy?

Electric just shrugs. "i'm entitled to have whatever i like," he sez. "it's just what i like, that's all."

an now Electric's rattling on about sum girl or other who's the daughter of sum one he knows in Wednesbury an he's like cupping his hands an going: "great little tits, know what i mean? i'd like to get a look at them little tits." he stands up momentarily just so he can thrust his crotch forward, screwing up his face. "i tell you. i'd love to stick me cock between them beauties." an from the way he's talkin i get a feelin sum thing ain't quite right w/his manner, sumthin just sounds right off cuz the girl's father is like only 32 years old or sumthin stupid so i go: "an about how old is this little vixen, man?"

Electric shakes his head, forking sum peas into his mouth. "how'm i sposed to know? bout 13, i guess. absolutely pristine at that age aren't they? firm as fuck."

"holy fuck," Amy goes. "she's... like... just a little fuckin kid, you freaky piece a shit!"

"on paper, yes. on paper," Electric nods. "but you ain't seen them bubs, man!"

"the *what*?" Amy frowns intensely, only half a bemused smile.

"the *bubs*!" Electric goes, forming shapes w/his hands. "y'know, the titties, the knockers, the puppies. the fuckin BAZOOKAS!"

thing is, you see, Electric weren't originally from Birmigham. it's like he's in a state of arrested development. he lived out in the wilds, sum tiny village an only moved to the city when his parents came to work at the big M&B brewery place after their farm sum where in Derbyshire went belly up. he went to this backwater school where his nickname was Grunty Pig. that was when he was 15 so i suspect his earliest sexual experiences was w/farmyard animals. so all tho he's in sum kinda state of arrested development little *human* girls are actually a step in the right direction -- for him. he's moved up a notch in terms of normality.

the waiter's lookin over at us down his black-haired nose like he just wants us the fuck outta the joint. he's lucky tonight becuz we decide to pay the bill since we're all too ossified to pull off a successful runner.

in the Black Horse the first thing i see when we walk in is that twat Disco Dave sittin on a stool, slumped over the bar totally fucked-up, his big silver wings of hair wet w/beer an it looks like he puked up all over himself. gone an fallen off the wagon. again. if he was ever actually on it.

derz a bunch a student losers playin darts in the main room so we grab sum drinks an then proceed to sit spazzed out in the corner by the pool-table in the shit-hole back room. there's empty bottles all over the floor an strips a torn wallpaper hang from the damp walls. there's sum hunch-shouldered anomaly sittin on a stool in there on his own, staring at the red tiled floor an drinkin a bottle a Becks an he's bin busted up bad. he's totally bruised up black an blue an swollen grotesquely an he's just got this thick congealed blud all over his face that his long, lank brown hair is all stuck to. he sed his name was Guss an he was dolefully tellin everyone bout how sum deal went bad up in Leeds an sum dudes smashed him up w/lead pipes an robbed his money out on a service station parking lot at 2 a.m.

Electric is clenching his teeth an sweating profusely an he just keeps repeating that he's havin a bad trip an blaming the shit i sell for it. *No Mercy* by L.A. Guns is blastin out the juke box but i got vapour trails in my eyes an the only dancing i do is tryna get to an from the toilets until the ginger-nut bouncer comes strolling up an i see him comin an i'm thinkin oh fuck, here we go again. sure enough he angrily grabs our drinks off us an tells us we all gotta leave immediately an fact a the matter is we're all too polluted w/drink an chemicals to be anythin other than all soft an compliant, so we're walkin out the joint quietly but just as we're leaving throo the front door Electric spews up bright orange puke all over the steps. "have *that,* you bastards," he shouts, laughing deliriously an givin them the v's throo the winnders.

we make it across town, superfucked out our heads. Electric trots along side us as we walk down Holt Street back into the city centre again an then in a moment of lucidity goes, "aaah, shit. hope i ain't puked up an undisolved acid tab."

it's still only like 7 p.m. i'm dragging Amy along w/me who's so zonked she can barely walk an that's hard becuz i can't even feel my own bodyweight. we cut fine figures throo the streets, bathed in the serene blue evening hue permeating the city as we scoot over to

Sinatra's bar for more drinks before heading up to the Hummingbird to get totally smashed again an at this point it feels like time has stopped an the night is gonna last forever.

# 8

some people are so loved up on life they see the beauty in every little thing. aahhh, the *music* of a fly buzzing about the room as you lie in bed tryna get sum sleep. but not me. i don't see such beauty. i get outta bed an roll up my copy a the NME from jan 1986 w/Andy Warhol an Debbie Harry on the cover an wait for the fly to land on the winnder sill before swatting the bastard dead.

    this was to be an Electric free day. he's apparently gone on a so called gin cruise on a narrowboat down the cut. beautiful sunrise of amber mixed w/blud red tendrils oozin from it across a fervent sky. i'm tellin you, it's like sum body sum where is pulling all the strings from the shadders, makin every body dance to their tune. the little Dinky-toy street-cleaning trucks were scuttling about, their yeller lights flashin manically as their spinnin brushes swept the pavements. all over town people were already out on the streets hustlin throo life, marchin off to work like little wind-up tin soldiers carryin their take-out coffees to their offices an production lines to rubber-stamp meaningless bits a paper, to knock nails into pieces a wood, to sit at sum pounding machine an press a big red button all day. beneath such skies how can we go on living such uninspired, mediocre lives?

people disintegrating right before your eyes, eaten away by it all. an you might look around an ask yourself time an time again why are people so bitter an unhappy? while the answer is clear: the effect of a corporate controlled media on malleable minds an ruptured spirits in a world where mass public opinion is the tyranny of our time. it's all gone wrong, man. society has all gone wrong. but in observance of people you can never look at such perfunctory constructs as their religions or their politics. you only look at how human nature attempts to use those ideologies as tools to get what it wants, which is in every case - power an control. society does not diversify to facilitate your weaknesses an failures; either as an individual, or as a demographic. if you remember that then people become better in your eyes becuz you just know we are all only at the mercy of it all.

an i ain't no religious man. i ain't no Jesus freak. when i drink red wine it's *red wine* not no proverbial blud a Christ an when i eat bred it's bred not no flesh a the messiah neither an there ain't no transubstantiation goin on inside me an if other people were the same as me the world'd be a better place. for them life is all fucked up, man. it's all like sum kinda personal sacrifice in order to preserve the group ideology becuz the group ethos is more important than the individual an it's like the sacraficial goat onto which the sins a the people are placed. but i'll tell you now for nuthin, i ain't gonna be sacraficing no goats either.

    things aren't at all complicated in the end. in the end, everythin is pretty simple: the idea is to sterilize society into antiseptic similitude. but the dissolution of hierarchies simply paves the way for a new, more stringent one to take root. an once the next religious empire is restored, make no mistake; they will force everyone under threat of death to comply w/their own definition of humankind. at first it will develop slowly, incrementally. an then, finally it will happen so abruptly it will seem like it came upon you overnight. western society is killin its youth. an one mornin you're gonna wake up to watch the fires burn. oh yeah. the new religious totalitarians are comin. the boys are back in town. an they're gonna kick your sorry matriarchal, feminised asses into kingdom come.

    so if you're sum socialist revolutionary an you tear down the hierarchy you're just throwing live ammunition on the bonfire so just get ready for a new one to establish itself an don't never think this time it's gonna be a wholesome or better one becuz it never is. it never fuckin is becuz no matter creed or culture it's a downright human frailty that only the psychopaths ever rise to the top an when that ammunition goes off you got no idea who gonna get hit.

truth is when you work in those stinkin factories or penned into those little office cubicles like sheep you measure out your life only in the time between cigarettes as you fall apart, dividing into subatomic particles. life becomes just a series of mechanical circumstances an in the end everything about your original personality expires, you're so soul-destroyed even love becomes just a transient delusion. only one thing is certain which is that you end up w/no need for love or work or friends or music, nuthin at all. you have no need for anything. all you want is to lie in bed an stare at the grey ceiling. an when they got you to that point, your mind becomes easily malleable. they take your youth away in school, hammer your individual purpose in life out of you, then they destroy the best years of your adult life w/mind-numbing relentless slavery of menial work you don't give 2 shits about. by the time you're too frail to do much they'll throw you a bone an leave you alone to live out your final few years.

there's no such thing as a factory floor

hero. there's just these faceless fuckers hidden away sum where behind corporate logos an government walls tryna run every body's lives, an if an element of insurrection runs throo your bludstream they'll rip the veins right out your flesh. but one day sum body gonna come along an start a real revolution, sum body who won't fall in line an get under the kosh gonna start puttin silver bullets in the hearts a monsters.

but it's sum days that are simple as this: you're walking throo the city a millions in the daytime toked up on amphets an you feel like a god w/all the motherfuckers around you, an you're not lookin for anyone an you don't need no one. that's the real deal, man. that's the purest kind a power there is.

the winnders in all the buildings ablaze w/the gold of the sun where all the pigeons line the winnder sills flapping their wings. an i sit looking out the winnder havin my morning coffee an smoke, an i wonder. i wonder if things like pigeons ever think about the nature of their circumstances, like do they think... well this it, man. this is the deal you bin handed, you are a pigeon an there is nuthin you can do about it. do any of the people think about it any more than the pigeons do? i'll tell you now for nuthin, drugs are not the contagion. drugs are the antidote.

Amy's still lyin in bed. i'm feeling pretty

lethargic but later this morning after i get Amy up an outta my hair i'm bussing over to see Slant Eye Joe. i gotta speak to him about our bouncer friend who confiscated/stole the tin of E's.

Slant Eye Joe runs a sleazeball massage parlour/brothel called the China Dolls House over on Pershore Street in Chinatown, which in any case serves only as a front for his drug empire but the fact remains you can get oiled up, massaged an fucked by 2 stunning 19 yr old Chinese birds there for like 200 quid a pop an he don't usually get bothered by the law cuz half the police force in Birmingham are gettin it free there. Slant Eye Joe is sum kind a mr. bigstuff in Chinatown. i mean he's like the King of Pussy, man. i can't profess to know what Slant Eye will do about that shitlord bouncer, i only know this: those tabs were like 1500 quid of his money an like i tried to warn him, he's gonna regret taking those pills, he ain't gonna enjoy the repurcussions. Slant Eye also owns the flat i'm living in. in fact, he owns the whole row a buildings in Hill Street, it's nuthin too glamourous but for as long as i'm doing a bit a dealing he lets me live here on the cheap.

got my walkman on. got my earphones in. listening to the Stooges 1$^{st}$ lp. but i pull out my plugs to hear what's goin on becuz upstairs on the bus people sit in silent laughter as a totally smashed out of his skull big ginger-headed Scottish geezer staggers up an down the aisle yelling: "ah, she's bin aff hoorin the nicht an ah fucken hate hoors. she's all fur coot an nae knickers!" you can see every body's shoulders jerking as they just keep their eyes to the floor becuz if you look up an catch his eye he flaps his fingers at you, calling you towards him an goes: "aye, come at me ya fluffy-puff wee jobby cunt, see what foor!"

as usual i gotta meet Slant Eye in a boozer called the Jeweller's Arms over in the Jewellery Quarter part a the city. an by the way, he's not even called Slant Eye cuz he's a Chink. in fact, i can tell you the date when he started gettin called that becuz i still got my ticket stub saved in a photo album w/all my other gig tickets. 9th a March, 1986. i was 19. i'd just got back from seeing Sigue Sigue Sputnik play the Powerhouse on Hurst Street when i got the call from one a Slant Eye's heavies who called to tell me to keep my eyes peeled for who's about. earlier that evening Slant Eye Joe was sittin outside his China Doll House at the wheel of his black XJ6 when one of a nigger gang from Lozells who call themselves the C.I.A walked up an shot him point blank straight throo the winnder. got hit 3 times in the head. he survived but lost his right eye an it kinda left his face on the slant where the slug busted his cheekbone all up. but whilst Slant Eye survived, whoever it was that did it, didn't. he an his family died couple a weeks later in a house fire. i remember sum time later after the heat cooled down asking Slant Eye – sum what naively really - if he did it. Slant Eye's like 50 years old at this point, an i remember he pulled this dour expression an put his hand on his heart an sed tepidly, "it hurts me that you'd ask that. it breaks my heart to see that kinda thing happen to a kid an his young family."

"them poor little kids," he added. an then he laughed.

today Slant Eye's wearing a black Italian slim-cut suit an his now customary patch over his shot out eye like he's Emilio Largo outta Thunderball but he don't wear a tie w/his suit he wears this glittering diamond brooch thing pinned at the neck of his pristine white shirt. he looks slim, fit an polished like Bruce fuckin Lee but the thing that gets me is the gunshot wound left a scar on his forehead an all an it makes him look a right evil fucker cuz it's kind a like a squiggle that looks like sum kinda occult symbol carved into his skin, it's like this upside down cross w/half moon cresecent over it an 2 dots each side an it looks like it means sum thing.

we sit down at a table in the corner of the Jeweller's away from the rest of the mid-day customers who're all jewellers an diamond dealers an shit like that from the whole surrounding Jewellery Quarter. lot a money around here. dirty money much of it, i'm guessing. there's a few small-time hustlers an all. an since Slant Eye always has me meet him in this joint i imagine he has his finger in sum pie over here probably w/the big dealer boys, the Jews. he got his fingers in almost everything right across Birmingham City.

all eyes in the place keep flitting in his direction every now an then. they all know Slant Eye, he's like this celebrity around here an everyone's shit scared of him but at the same time they all kind a suck up to him. for instance, there's this little man at the bar known as Diamond Derek who's got a hunch back an a kind a crooked hip an sorta crabs along the street sideways back an forth between his shop an the pub. he gives a deferential nod an wink every time he catches Joe's eye. there's also Bob the Gob. he's just sum boring bastard who likes to talk about politics an the less sed about him the better.

"you might be a lot a things, Mark" Slant Eye says. he's got one a those new Nokia P4000 mobile phones that he pulls out his pocket an puts on the table. "but i like you becuz one thing you've always bin w/me is 100% on the level." he puts his hand on my shoulder an adds, "you leave this motherfucker to me. after i've spoken to him he'll know he's bin spoken to." an then Joe frowns momentarily, like thinkin bout sum thing really hard an he leans right back in his chair an goes, "by the way, did this thieving coon say anything to you when you told him the goods belong to me."

"yeah, he sed you can kiss his ass."

Slant Eye's face takes on a weird sort a bemused contortion like you were pinching his ear, he's just not accustomed to the disrespect, an he goes, "*what?*"

"he sed you can kiss his ass." i scratch my nose nervously, look away.

"are you kidding me? he sed that about... *me?* not *you?*"

"yeah yeah, Joe, he meant you!" i'm even laughing a little bit while i'm trying to tell him cuz Joe just can't believe it an his face is a picture an i'm stabbing the table w/my index finger to drive the point: "i told him catagorically those mints belong to Slant Eye Joe an if he knows what's good for him he'll give em me back. but he laughed in my face an sed you can go down there yourself an kiss his big black booty - those were his exact words: you can kiss his big. black. booty. he slapped his own backside to make the point an everythin. an ohhh yeah... somethin else for good measure, he called you a ping-pong, pan-faced chinksta."

Slant Eye unbuttons his suit jacket an shifts position in his chair, crosses his legs in a relaxed manner. financially speaking, Joe ain't gonna give a shit about a pissy little 2 grand but he ain't gonna like this kind a disrespect. Slant Eye considers me suspiciously throo squinted eyes, tapping the table w/his glossy manicured finger nails for a long time, his head cocks to one side, then says: "fuck me backwards, you're telling the truth." Slant Eye sipped his drink an continued, "you know there comes a point in life we only find out what we're made of when we're forced to taste our own blood... i think the time has come for this ratchet-ass motherfucker to taste his."

i nod an continue a little awkwardly, "thing is, Joe," i say. "that asswipe piece a crap is gunner of sold them pills or sum shit like that. now this puts me in a difficult financial position. that money's gone. i'm broke. can i get some gear -- on the tick, like?"

Slant Eye waves his hand, diamond rings on his fingers flashing in the light, an smiles an says, "i'll look after you. i'll have one a the fellas drop you some shit round later this evening. Chinese take-away style. make sure you're in. same deal as ever, you already know my cut an whatever you can get on top is yours. you can pay me when you've sold it."

after we finish the Remy Martin XO's Slant Eye's bought us we go outside to his fire-truck-red Rolls Royce Corniche an he gives me a ride home. as we go past the big Kumar clothing warehouse place heading back into the city centre an as we glide around St. Chad's Island, past the West End Bar, Slant Eye goes to me, "i'm just curious, you still messing about w/that bird?"

"which one?" i say.

"y'know very well which one. that mental bitch in the Converse All-Stars," he sez. "that girl is so chemical if you stuck her in a blender you could use the remains as industrial cleaner."

"Amy," i nod. "yeah she still comes around, you know."

Slant Eye raises his finger, nods sagely an goes, "you wanna get ridda that Chuck Taylor rancid whore. she's bad news, kiddo."

"well, you have to understand her, know what i mean? she's a woman of raw emotions." i don't even know why i'm sayin it, i make the stupid excuse for myself more than i do Amy.

"woman of raw emotions, eh? Christ, will you just listen to yourself?" Slant Eye says. "i'm just tellin you as a friend, kid. you stay w/a woman like that she'll drive you mad, you gonna end up stabbin your own eyeballs out. she's bad, bad, bad news. i'm sure she fucks like a rattlesnake but take away the fucking an what's a girl like that good for? tell me, what's a girl like that good for?"

i shake my head an consider the question for a long time before i shrug awkwardly an offer: "i suppose she's just one a them morose, disturbed women – she's got a split personality an she don't know what she wants."

"you're fuckin tellin me!" Slant Eye goes. "listen, you wanna girl? i'll send you a nice Chinese girl." an Slant Eye adjusts his eyepatch an laughs an adds, "who'll love you long time."

"ah," i say. "Amy just gets a wild hare up her ass about things sum times."

but there is a certain truth in my life an that is that i've always been an outsider. i have been rejected an excluded to the point that i don't have feelings either way for anyone anymore. in my life people come an people go. it ain't up to me, they can do as they please an my numbness lends me a kind of emotional immunity. i'll never be part of the mass. eventually you just don't give a shit. but as detached as one may seem there will always be the bleeding of old wounds. on occasions, there will always be the opening up of old wounds. the world is relentless an in the end it always prevails over us. one day the molecules that hold everything together will dissolve an one day you're just gone from this realm an sum body comes along an clears the shit out your house an sum body else moves their shit in, everything carries on an nobody gives a fuck. an even within your own family it don't matter much. you're just about an unknown quantity an 2 generations down the line you're just a genetic sequence in the bloodline.

there's a clear blueness to the sky i haven't seen in a while an it looks beautiful. it's blue like a sapphire. we continue on in silence, Roxy Music's *Do the Strand* just sounds so great playing on Slant Eye's super expensive Burmester car stereo.

Slant Eye's Roller pulls to halt outside my gaff an i get out. the staff in the neighbouring shops along the row are peering out the winnders, stretching their necks, watching me, wondering what my story is. they never much liked the look a me... but now, now it's like: who is this young kid? they're asking themselves, good-looking boy an he knows sum pretty bigwig people to boot!

i stand on the footpath an spark up a cigarette before strolling leisurely w/easy grace across the road to my door like i own this goddamn city. the dark haired girl who works in the newsagents is standing in her doorway. i wink an say simply, "alright?" an she goes, "yeah, are you?" an i go, "sound...as a pound." an i stick the key in my door like it's the door to a palace.

# 9

it's early Saturday mornin an Electric, Superfast an me are walkin down Bull Street headin to a café for a big breakfast fry-up when Superfast yells. "there's that little poison fuckin dwarf who robbed me!" an sure enough we see the Big D standing on the pavement wearin a fuckin tuxedo an top hat doin magic tricks w/cards an scarves an plastic flowers. he sees us an grabs his begging cap an bolts, leavin all his gear behind on the floor. as we're chasing after him Superfast goes, "i don't give a fuck if he's a dwarf, i'm gonna kick the fuck out the thieving pikey bastard." Big D runs all the way onto Corporation Street all the time shouting "HELP! HELP!" but a course no body gives a fuck, no body takes a blind bit a notice. his top hat flies off an a load a plastic ping pong balls an shit spills out of it as he disappears down the steps to the deserted subway like a rabbit down a hole an Superfast is running out ahead of us going, "holy christ he's pissin like a racehorse!" an a course the Big D must be like 190lbs an all, which is pretty fucking colossal for sum one who's like 3 an a half foot tall but his tiny legs are going like a little chopping pair a scissors, the kid is like a Cheetah, man.

we eventually manage to catch him down in the subway when Superfast gives him a mega smack round the back a the swede, sending the Big D sprawlin down on his face. he rolls onto his back an makes a feeble attempt to pull out a Stanley knife but i stand on his wrist an kick it out his hand. his body's all blubbery an hard at the same time an it's like kicking a sack a garbage as we lay the boot in. "where's my fuckin tenner, you thieving little gypsy cunt?" Superfast spits, leaning down into Big D's face, who's now lying flat on his back bathed in the murky yeller subway lights.

"i'm sorry aren't i?" Big D whimpers. "needed the money, y'know how it is, yeh yeh?" an then he adds sumwhat matter-a-factly, "an i ain't even a gypsy anyway."

"i don't give a fuck what you are. give us the tenner now, you horrible little bastard," i tell him. "or we'll kick the livin shit outta you, i swear."

" i ain't got it, yeh yeh? but i can get it. i can get it." he's sittin up on the damp, dirty floor now restin back on his hands an we're standin around him. "that's all i got, honest," Big D whimpers, nodding towards the cloth cap he opens up an he's got about a quid in there all in shrapnel.

we give the lying little shit a bit more of a kicking an a few punches, nuthin too bad, we're pulling our punches really, we still got hearts after all, just enough to teach him a lesson, an begin to walk away but as we leave him there sittin cryin on the floor he got the audacity to blurt out after us, "you bunch a fuckin queerboys." becuz that's what happens when you show a simpering, sorry little asshole a bit a mercy. now you really got to admire such defiance in a man but that don't mean it can't go unpunished an i got my Dr. Martens on so i go back an boot him straight in the face, knocking him down on his back, his disgusting blubbery milk-white stomach w/black hairs sprouting out of it sticking out from under his grey tshirt heavin up an down. he's gurgling blud from his mouth an nose an at this point I hear him shit himself an a big wet stain a brown diarrhoea seeps throo his shorts an i reckon that's lesson enough for him now. before i walk away i tell him: "don't steal money off people, it's not very nice." an i waggle my finger at him an go sarcastically "...yeh yeh?" an he shakes his head an goes, "yeh yeh, i won't do it again." but a course you know very well he will becuz he's the livin manifestation of the proverbial little poison dwarf.

    we go back above ground an get outta the area swift as we can. we scramble up to Colmore Circus Queensway where we hang around a bit w/our hands in our pockets. Electric sez flatly, "well, that was just fuckin surreal, man. quite literally kickin the shit out a *dwarf*!"

    we decide we better dispense w/breakfast an break up in case the chickenlivered little bastard calls the fuzz an gives them sum spiel about how *we* robbed *him.*

    myself, i grab a hot-dog from a stand that's

set up on Temple Row an head off home. spend the rest a the day sprawled on my bed smokin sum Buddha grass an listenin to the Spacemen 3.

trying to get to sleep later that night, i don't feel good about beatin up that little shit Big D, it's kind a playin on my conscience. but it was a heat a the moment thing i keep tryna tell myself, an however you wanna look at it he was a thieving little bastard. but even so, now in the cold light a day it's weighing on my mind, his face when i kicked him in it, the awful thud. causing a grown man to walk home w/his pants full a shit. but he asked for it. he fuckin asked for it, i keep telling myself. but still, it was only a tenner – an truth is, it weren't even *my* tenner.

yeah. he was still a thieving little cunt though.

\* \* \*

this time i cram 50 disco biscuits in an Elvis Presley pez dispenser i found on the flea market for 50p an keep the rest a the tabs at home until Elvis requires a refill. i also got 100 gram wraps a white lightning ready to go an a sheet of 250 acid tabs. true to his word, one a Slant Eye's boys dropped the gear off at about 8pm that evening, Chinky take-away delivery van marked up Hung Larj Chinese Restaurant - that name is Slant Eye Joe's little joke - pulled up outside an delivered the gear in 2 tin foil trays inside a brown paper bag. i'm right back in the saddle. after subtracting Slant Eye's cut i make over 2 grand on this consignment an i'll offload this lot within a week, less a few hits for myself.

i never drink in the Dome nightclub, it's a chickenshit cheesefest where the music is chart disco bullshit but it's a big club that holds like a few thousand dipshit clubbers all looking for momentary escape from their dreary factory-floor lives so i'm going down there to flog sum gear to the chickenshits who frequent the place. i'm thinkin i can get 12 quid a tab for acid an E down there cuz they're all kind a desperate an they'll happily pay a little over. one thing you always got to remember is that for most people life is over-rated an drugs an drink are a cheap line in fantasy, the anaesthetic that numbs you from the anguish. if you could live in those nightclubs, cocooned from the outside world forever, you would. you definitely would. an you'd die there in bliss in that glittering make-believe world just so you never have to go to your shitstain jobs.

it's a total deluge out there an i'm in a bar along Temple Row watching the bleak sheets of grey rain sweeping across St. Philips Cathedral an there's a hot-dog stand on the corner bellowing glowing white steam into the black dusky atmosphere an the drenched hot-dog guy w/plastic carrier bag wrapped round his head. but a little before 9 p.m the rain yields an all that's left is the black sky an dripping buildings so i bang back my Jack Daniel's an get off on my way to the Dome.

Temple Street is a narrow conduit that slices between Temple Row an New Street an cutting throo i bump into these 4 straggle-haired student kids i know right outside the Sputnik bar who're all from the uni campus.

like it's sum sorta Birmingham University uniform 2 of the dweebs are in their ripped Levis an Doc Martens an they got on Sonic Youth an Dinosaur Jr tshirts an threadbare green cardigans thinkin they're Kurt Cobain or sum body but Olsen's wearin a Beatles tshirt an i poke him in the stomach playfully an say sarcastically, "nice tshirt, Olsen." Olsen rolls backwards an goes, "hey, the Beatles influenced everyone, man. all pop music can be chronologically related back to them!" an i go, "yeah yeah, all pop music can be related back to them - just like e-coli germinates in sum body's bowel sum where."

they're just a bunch a stupid drongo uni kids, i spose just hangin around an drifting throo their days lookin for sum thing an nuthin in life.

Olsen's this weird kid, man. like he's sum

lefty liberal pinko slacker bastard, member of the student union an all that crap, you know the type, priding themselves on fighting for everybody's rights an all that ineffectual stuff that just don't matter at all, digesting an then regurgitating what he's bin fed by purveyors of bullshit left wing politics, people who just don't understand how human nature works, don't understand the human animal cuz they bin suckerpunched by Marxist ideology. he pretends to be one a those power to the people fuckers w/Che Guevara posters on his bedroom wall that will stand on street corners parroting crap maxims like "95% of the wealth is owned by the richest 5%" an he acts all insipid like he's sum gay bender homo faggot. but i don't even think he is homo, i think he's just on some pretentious weird kind a faggot trip cuz he thinks it's a more evolved way to be like he believes himself to be sum kind a enlightened being or sum thing. truth is, he's a total gimp. an he's gone an had his hair cut in this shit kinda quiff / Mohican hybrid thing an it totally looks like the haircut of despair. i suspect one a these days Olsen's gonna end up alone an he's gonna be found one day standing staring throo the winnder of a ladies' lingerie shop, licking the glass an they'll come along an go "let's go motherfucker" an they'll cart him off an shut him away.

    but i digress, people can change over time.

he seems like a nice enough kid who's just totally bewildered about the world around him, poor bastard's been fed a diet a bullshit an instead a thinkin for himself he's just swallowed it. seems to me that they got you formulating no thoughts of your own an you end up just this fuckin stupid little echo chamber spouting maxims, surrogate ideologies implanted in your mind throo your television an newspapers. but all this shit is like it's bin planned, man. only the patriarchy has ever protected nations an it's like first they socially engineer a nation of emasculinated insipid males an then a new patriarchy moves in an kicks everybody's asses into kingdom come an it's just a walkover cuz derz not enough real men left to fight the onslaught. these kids think it's sum kinda evolution of man but it ain't no evolution, they turned you into a moron voting for the very people who're gonna put you in the ground, it's like cows voting for the slaughterman.

straight away they ask if i'm carrying sum thing nice so i tell them sure as shit i am, an i sell them sum E's for a tenner a pop. as they hold out their hands i go click click click click w/the Elvis Presley pez dispenser an w/each click i go, "uh huh... uh huh... uh huh... uh huh" as Elvis spits the tabs out his mouth into their palms an the kids laugh an hand over the lettuce which i fold an zip up safe in my leather biker jacket breast pocket. truth is they think i'm their friend but i'm nobody's friend, i just go throo a series of mechanical actions that friends might do. an in truth i think secretly most people do that too. we are all dysfunctional in our own respective ways cuz the truth is we're all carrying our own cross around inside ourselves, we all just hide it, that's all. as the group heads off into Sputnik 1 of them, this young kid called Beezy, pops his tab an says, "i've always said drugs keep you young an healthy right up until the day you die!" an i go, "yeah, Beezy... at the age of 25."

the kids ask me if i got time for a swifty w/them in Sputnik's an i'm like yeah i always got time for a quick one so we go down the stairs into yet another city centre basement bar where you just know if there's a fire you ain't never gonna make it out an you'll be incinerated alive down there. 1 of them, i dunno which one, gets the round a drinks in an i'm standin there w/my whisky watchin this indie trio who're first on the bill tonight an i think the name's sposed to be ironic or sum thing cuz they've called themselves Vasectomize the Poor an they're really just tryna be the Smiths or sum thing like that, singin all this pseudo-political bullshit like eat the fuckin rich an sum load a boring crap about the partisan divide, whatever the fuck they think that is. it's all that kind a shit you hear lefty-liberal commie bastard uni students spouting off about all the time. singer's got sum a them chac-chacs that he keeps shakin an it's goin *sha sha sha sha sha shaaaaa* an i say to Olsen, "what the fuckin hell is this crap, man?"

"it's powerful political comment, Mark." Olsen informs me, kind a sniffin an lookin down his middle-class nose at me. he thinks i don't know his parents are loaded, but i do know. i can tell kids like him a mile away. i know he goes back home to his parent's Surrey fuckin mansion during holidays. all this type a student union crap, it's just a bullshit middle class person's approximation of working class socialism an i can see straight throo his pretensions. joint is full of em, in fact. just a bunch of indie kids in torn jeans an Sonic Youth, Faith No More an Nirvana tshirts hangin around all listless an lank haired like it's a competition to see who can look the most bored an disinterested. an it don't matter none where you go, it's the same shit just a different town. but these kids are like 19, you know. sucked into all that university pinko politics; they're been indoctrinated, not educated. the champagne-socialists of the future. it's always the same old jive; people who don't know shit gobbing off.

the 2nd band up on stage are this death-metal band, Benediction an they are fuckin heavy, man. heavier than Megadeth or Slayer. they sound pretty alright. the singer's about 10 foot fuckin tall an if he duz 1 a them jumps again he's gonna hit his head on the roof. the guitarist is good, just stands there w/his legs spead like he's holdin a machine gun an shooting off into crescendos to form off-kilter time signatures. i mean, he's gunning us down, man. "oh yeah!" the Olsen kid tells me, "these motherfuckers sold like 50,000 albums."

i stand about a while finishing my drink an despite the fact i like the band i got more important business to see to.

even at this time a night the soul-savers are out. on a corner there's sum religious idiot waving a bible about. he's babbling sum batshit crazy stuff at the top of his voice about burning bushes, sticks turning into snakes an god transmorgrifying people into pillars of salt or stone or whatever the fuck. he's relating sum story an gets to the bit about Balaam an his donkey, an animal which god himself apparently blessed w/the ability of speech an i'm thinking: talk about talking out your ass. you can't never let these religious idiots gain any ground. you can never let them win.

funny thing. all i can really remember about being a kid is the total confusion, looking around an not understanding anything an my overtly religious adopted parents imbued w/religious invective not being able to explain any of it to me outside of sum biblical claptrap. took me a long time to start making sense a the world on my own terms as i saw it.

i can hear music thumping from the Dome at like half a mile away an its lights are illuminating the sky above, these beams of yeller an blue light shooting up into the black night, scanning the sky an you look an it's like you'd expect to see the Batman logo. outside i stand just around the corner of the building an the first customer of the night is sum young poodle haired kid who looks a right dweeb in sum sort a wide-shouldered zoot suit that's black w/white arms an he's wearin it w/silk naked pin-up girl tie. "that last acid you sold me was *mega!*" the kid says. "i mean like i saw real *goblins* climbing up out the *drains*!" i don't remember the kid at all but i slap him on the arm an go, "hey, if it's real to you it's money to me."

i'm gettin the punters going in, keepin way out a sight of the overzealous bruisers on the door at this joint who're thick as 2 short fuckin planks but think themselves hot shit real cops or sum thing on a mission an it's not even becuz they want to to keep the city clean from people like me, they're really just on a power trip an they're tryna impress the girls. i recognise one a the doorman, he's worked a few a the doors all over town. he can only be described as primitive. a more primitive 2 braincell stripe of human being. he's this big white fuckin knucklehead body builder type a goon who calls himself Nimbo for whatever stupid reason an he thinks he's Ivan Drago.

i watch as a blonde in a short flimsy dress heads towards the door an the big lumbering pillock grabs his crotch an bounces up an down excitedly an goes, "hey, Sally how's about comin round the back an givin Nimbo a bit a yer sugar?" the girl sweeps past him givin him the finger an says, "here's a better idea - why don't you bend over an suck it yourself, but don't suck too hard you might suck your brains out, you bozo."

as yet i got no clue how true it is, people are so fulla shit but i get word from one a the regular clubbers from the Hummingbird who's heading in here tonight that Superfast dropped dead in the place last night. collapsed on the dancefloor comatose, went into hypoventilation an got carted off in the meat wagon. this does not come as a complete shock to me. sounds to me like he must a misjudged the amount of the opioid mix in his speedballs again. he's done that before an got stomach pumped or sum thing. his eyes were always bigger than his belly. an if it's true, this time it was fatal.

i kinda don't believe it tho. perhaps it's like a defence mechanism of mine or sumthin but i dunno why i think these things at times like this but i got an image in my head of a little cartoon caricature of Superfast lying on the floor w/tongue sticking out an 2 little + + for eyes.

i've offloaded about half the gear i'm carryin when a police patrol car drifts past slowly an i can see the 2 cops scoping me out. the car goes up to the traffic island where i know they're gonna spin a full 180 an come back towards me so as soon as i'm in his blindspot i scamper across to the Greek restaurant across the road an go inside. i buy just an Ouzo by itself an sit down by the winnder, skulking behind the curtains. i watch the cop Jag prowl past slowly looking for me an then its red tail lights blend into the stream of jostling traffic along Bristol Street. but i'm pretty happy w/the evening's business so i don't further risk it for the rest of the night, i finish my drink an make my way home, the hot aniseed of the Ouzo warming my chest even though i can feel the cold closing in around me.

en route i buy a newspaper from a macerated old hunchback at a street stand who stinks a drink an is mumified by a woolly hat an scarf wrapped round his face. back at my place i pour a whisky an randomly flip throo the paper. there's sum piece about this sicko teen on the northside a the city who lost his virginity to his mother's corpse after killing her. the dumb shit writer of the piece makes a connection between that an the teen's obsession w/Black Sabbath an Judas Priest an a loada bullshit about how that meant he was into black magic an shit like that an the writer dropped in words like "bizarre" an "ritual" an "blood" an "homosexual" – all sensationalist words intended to invoke emotional responses in the tabloid-mind of readers who do not actually apply any cognitive thought to the bullshit they're digesting.

i light a cigarette an sit pretty zonked out by the winnder, turning things over in my mind. man, this world, it's like a sea of bullshit you gotta swim in. the sky is jewelled w/bright chromium stars an i dunno why people do the things they do, i only know sum one a 1000 years ago would a looked up at that sky an seen the same moon i'm lookin at right now. everything has the illusion of permanence. but in 200 years all this will be gone, the city unrecognisable from its current condition, all these lives around me gone an forgotten, everything altered, relocated or replaced. the only recognisable things as i know them today will be all these corporate logos, immortal, glowing like religious symbols in the eyes of new generations.

i spose i'll find out if Superfast is really dead in the morning.

# 10

i never cared much for Gram Parsons. an he comes on the radio so i switch it off. i mean that shit's like music to die to. slow grey morning. drizzle against the winnder. waiting for my black Levi's to dry, spent an hour just staring in anodyne transfixion at the washing machine goin round an round. fell asleep for a little bit. later on, i looked in the kitchen cupboards for food an all i had in was sum tinned potatoes an a jar a peanut butter, so this afternoon while having a smoke of the old Buddha grass, before i headed out to the café for sum thing to eat, i watched an early 80s porno classic w/John Holmes an Ginger Lynn. it was about this girl who goes for a job interview an fucks the guy in his office to get the job an the scene all culminates in the money-shot when John Holmes cums in Ginger's mouth an when she spits an lets it dribble down her tits he goes, "hey, you spilled your lunch." which i thought was a stroke of comedic genius. but i'm not sure whether she got the job or not. i even hit the <<REWIND button an watched again but it still wasn't made totally clear. i think she probably did. i mean, it was a good performance, man. that girl just loved to fuck. i mean you'd definitely give her the job if you were the boss an knew you were gonna get that kind a head

on tap. i tell you, that guy's a fool if he didn't give her the job.

walkin up Stephenson Place, at the bottom a the New Street ramp that takes you up to the shopping mall/train station there's always sum full a shit group of sum sort w/a little table set up, preaching or collecting money for sum cause or whatever. last week when i walked past it was African men w/beards in long white robes handing out leaflets about the evil of the white race an babbling on about white devils an demons an God's ultimate plan regarding the establishment of a black planet when the evil whites are all extinguished an banished back to the hell from whence they came. sum crap like that anyway. how we whites are born evil an all got demonic blood shootin throo our veins. there was gonna be a few white devils allowed to stay alive, the females of whom were gonna be used for the sexual pleasure of their black masters an all the surviving insipid white men were gonna be enslaved to do all the manual labour whilst in these ideologues' world the black race would take their rightful place on de throne, lazing around as the natural lords an masters a planet earth, an as a result equilibrium would be restored to de planet, just like how de worl' was before whitey came along an gatecrashed the party.

conversely, today it's laughably sum equally deluded far right political movement i don't even know the name of who're like skinheads in black Harrington jackets an black combat trousers tucked into highly polished boots like they think they're sum kind a military unit. the big cheese of the group is addressing a small audience that has gathered around him an he's laying it all down flat out that we're a nation in the midst of committing genosuicide. "the blade has already been put to the vein," he's shouting vehemently, "the veins have already been cut," slicing a finger cross his wrist to illustrate his point, repeating the word genosuicide over an over. "now we're just waitin for the blood to drain from the wound." dramatic pause to let that sink in. then he adds: "but it's not too late to stem the flow... we are injured but not dead yet." his eyes are wild. "we're at a crossroads, brothers an sisters...." he sez.

an i dunno what the fuckadoodle is goin on in this city today but a little further along near the Rotunda derz another bunch a religious retarded mutant freaks from sum kind a Jesus church, they're dancing about an chanting an shit an one a them who thinks he's fucking Joseph or sum body in an oversized multi-coloured knitted cardigan is holdin up a placard that says sum fucking Christian hippy shit:

**IF YOU DON'T TEACH YOUR CHILDREN THE WORD OF GOD THE DEVIL WILL TEACH THEM :**
**MATHEMATICS**
**PSYCHOLOGY**
**EVOLUTION**
**GEOMETRY**
**PHYSICS**
**& WITCHCRAFT!!!**

i just got no clue what the score is. no idea what kind a fuckin bullshit they're tryna preach to everybody. you gotta look at all these people an say society's headin for sum big fuckin trouble. all these fuckers should be locked up in a mental home. it's like that slow Fun Boy Three song, *The Lunatics Have Taken Over the Asylum.*

dum da dum – dum da dum - ah-aaaah. ah-aaaah.

too many unsophisticated minds tryna take on the big ideas, their cognizance poisoned by articles of politics an dogma. i got no time for any a these ideologues an their bullshit, no matter what side a the political fence they're coming from. ideologues don't think cuz they ain't been educated to think, they been indoctrinated. it's like they got no middle finger. fuck em. only a life a hedonism in this sea of garbage is the answer to all this crap. everybody gotta stop givin a shit otherwise society gonna be in sum deep trouble, i'm tellin you. you gotta get out there an drink an smoke an listen to rock n roll becuz that's all your minds are sufficient for. i'm correlating the decline in society directly w/the erosion of youth culture by the powers that be throo insidious social engineering. an it's like all these student kids, man. the activists. these dweebs think they're fighting it but they been over-politicised, divided an conquered. they're just sum little shits who already been battered down like dogs an they don't even know it.

i wander around aimlessly for a while an then in Vagabond's on Hurst Street i buy a black shirt w/silver polka-dots an a big thick vintage leather belt with a big brass Boy's Brigade belt buckle.

\* \* \*

i'm not sure why i like it here. the gaff is a little decrepit an sad. i call it the Melancholy Café. but its real name, the Tulip Café on Hurst Street, couple a doors away from the big casino place, is quiet an empty today, except for this usual old neurotic guy who's in here all the time. his name's Marvin an he's like about 70 or sum thing, always sits at a table near the winnder, peering out over the top of the little blue gingham curtains, waiting for his wife. most heartbreakin thing i ever saw. his eyes are an empty ineffable Atlantic Ocean grey. lonely, searching, devastated eyes. there is pain etched into his face. his wife died 3 years ago but he sits there waiting. "oh i don't know what she's got up to," he says. "round the shops spending my money, i expect," he laughs. Marvin looks at his watch every 5 minutes an tuts an shakes his head an he keeps askin if you've seen his wife. they used to come in the café together but now he just comes in an sits an waits for her to turn up becuz his mind simply refuses to accept she is gone an every time the door opens he looks up hopefully. you can't help but wish you could take his lonliness away. i feel like offering him sum tranks, sum ludes or sum thing, to numb him from his inner pain but it'd probably be even more hurtful to deprive him of his self-sufficient delusion. fuckin shame, man. why does life have to be so cruel an pointless? why does life have to hurt people so much?

it's 3 p.m an outside it's already gettin dark, the skies are black an the rain is black an the streets are black. we are all under the light of a dying sun to the melancholy sound of a busker in the street outside singing *Ruby Tuesday* an playin a twenny quid junk-shop guitar.

derz a Slush Puppie machine in the café an Darkie the Dago, the owner a the place is always drinkin a big cup a the cherry flavour but you can always smell he's got a furtive dose a vodka mixed in there an his eyes are half-lidded w/mellow alcoholic gravity an his skin is pulled tight over his face an his awful tight, thin lips rather give him the look of a snake. i've seen that dead behind the eyes look in men before. somewhere along the line, he's been knifed by a woman. roses are red, but so is a pound a flesh.

Darkie's always got his little kid w/him in the place who's there so much it don't even look like he goes to school. he's this stumpy fat as a pig dago called Sebastian an all this kid ever seems to do is wail an cry an say, "i'm starving" an just to keep him quiet Darkie just keeps stuffing the greedy little bastard full a fried crap an chocolate an that's probably why he's gotten so fat that his cheeks are all puffed up so big that his eyes are just squinting mishapen slits but if the little bastard don't get what he wants he just bawls the place down. never seen a kid be able to eat so much. horrid child but you know how it is, customers in the joint smile an call him cute an pinch his ample cheeks even tho after eating all his own food he waddles about the place tryin to pick food off people's goddamn plates like a vulture. i'll bet you 100 quid he'll be dead from heart attack before the age a 30 and as far as i'm concerned that day can't come quick enough, do himself an us all a favour.

this world is full a motherfuckers. i'm tellin you. i order steak an chips an i sit down at a rickety table w/coffee an open the Birmingham Post dated October 17th 1991 at random an i'm reading this little piece about sum motherfucker called George Hennard in Texas who's shot 23 people dead in a Killeen city restaurant called Luby's yesterday. this motherfucker Hennard drove his pick-up throo the winnder an then started shootin w/a Glock an a Ruger.

but my eye is more keenly drawn to a smaller local piece below that story. not too much info yet. it says a bouncer at XLs nightclub has been shot dead in a motorbike drive-by. the paper don't yet reveal the dead bouncer's name. but a course i know his name. police looking for witnesses but so far as usual, nobody saw jack shit. an on occasions such as this most of that stuff is genuine – it ain't always just out a fear of reprisals that nobody will say nuthin, most a the time people are too stupid or self-absorbed to ever notice anything. but in any case, all the police got on it so far is that it was a jet black Kawasaki Ninja motorcycle. rider also dressed in all black leathers opened fire once w/Browning 9mm an hit the bouncer once in the head point blank, left his brains yeller, purple, red pretty like a rainbow spread up the wall in an arc before the Kawasaki peeled away slick as Batman on his bat-bike. course, paper didn't write that it was all pretty like rainbow, that's just my imagining of the scene. pretty like a rainbow - w/bits in it, i'd imagine. other bouncer thought it was a female rider cuz of the long silky black hair hanging out the back a the helmet. that's all they know. Mike the bozo died tasting his own blud at the scene long before the meat wagon even got there.

fuck, man. an that's why you don't tell Slant Eye Joe to kiss your black ass. or your white ass, for that matter, in case you're wondering. he don't kiss nobody's ass.

Darkie brings the steak an chips over to my table an i fold up the newspaper an toss it on the adjacent table. the food's pretty good. steak done in a pepper sauce, chips doused in goose fat or sum thing making them thick an crispy. Marvin smooths down his white hair, gets up from his chair looking at his watch an says he'd better get off an see if his wife has gone straight home. man, that just about brings tears to my eyes, man.

when i come out the café the busker outside is doing his own rendition of Led Zeppelin's *Ramble On.*


it's been a while since i saw Mad O'Leary. i run into him walking up Sherlock Street on my way to the Diskery to buy sum vinyl. Mad O'Leary's just sum young, pissed off punk who looks like he models himself on Colin Abrahall the lead singer of GBH w/bright blonde spike haircut except O'Leary can barely write his own name on his unemployment benefit application. Mad O'Leary's one a them kids who's a real life *Rebel Without a Cause*, it's like he just wants to tear the whole world a new asshole for no real reason at all. he sticks a cigarette between his lips an leans into me an talks furtively out the side of his all but toothless mouth:

"hey, you wanna buy sum pasties?" he sez.

an i'm like thinking pasty must be sum new word for sum kind a drug i've never heard used before an i go, "maybe, what they like?" an O'Leary sez, "yeh, man. they all good" an he opens up the hold-all he's got slung over his shoulder an shows me inside an i dunno what planet he lives on but true enough he's got a load a cheese an onion pasties still in their cellophane wrappers that he's nicked from Abdul's corner shop near where O'Leary rents a 1 room flat on Oxhill Road. he smiles this weird smile exposing the few teeth he has got an they're tiny an pointy, like you'd expect to see in the mouth of a piranha.

"nah, man, i'm stuffed," i tell him, stabbing a thumb over my shoulder. "i've just come out the fuckin café."

O'Leary pulls hard on his cigarette an blows out a jet a smoke. "thing is," he goes, lookin over his shoulders. "i could do wi'sum whizz an er… well the truth is, see i an't got no dough."

"same old, same old," i tell him, laughing as i playfully faux-reluctantly hand him a wrap. "you've never got no dough."

"ohh, shiiiit," he goes as i drop the little envelope in his grimy palm. "you're a star! i owe you one, bro!" he bounces up an down pumping his fist.

"yeah you owe me about a gazillion, you fuckin faggot!" i shout as i walk away. "wooo hooo," he goes.

problem w/Mad O'Leary is he always acts an talks like he knows sumthin about sum thing, like he's got the inside low-down on sumthin or other. he sez he knows who did the Birmingham pub bombings. but truth is he just talks an incalculable amount of nuthin, he just pulls the information out his ass, an problem is he's never got anythin better to do w/himself so given the chance he hangs around me too long givin me all his tiresome bullshit so if i tell him where i'm going right now he'll wanna tag along an i just can't be doing w/listening to his jabber. he's about as interesting as the shipping forecast.

* * *

at the Diskery i bought the 2 LPs i was planning on getting - the Cramps' *Smell of Female* an the

Miracle Workers' *Overdose.* but when i got there Sonic Boom, singer in the Spacemen 3 was hanging around in there so i also bought their *Recurring* LP an got him to sign it. he signed the gold cover in red pen an drew a little doodle, too.

i'm in my gaff settling in for the night, lookin at the record covers, readin the liner notes while i spin the vinyl on the Duel turntable when a tiny stone tinkles against the winnder so i go over an take a look out. couple a freak Mod kids in Parkas, Tripod an Hawkeye on their way to Kaleidoscope as usual, looking for a couple a tabs. they're ok kids but they're just a pair a shit-for-brains dweebs really, pair a little street urchins who know nuthin bout anythin an yet anythin seems to excite them. Hawkeye got that name cuz he's got a cock-eye that stares off at an angle an no matter where he looks it don't move at all it just stares fixed up an to the right. i got no idea whether he can actually see out the fucker, or if it's just dead in his skull. either way it's weird how he don't crash his Vespa when he's riding it.

Kaleidoscope's a pub just like 50 yards along the street from my gaff but i never bin in the joint, same as Sam Weller's round the other side a the building i live in, never been in there either. both a bit too close to home for my liking. Kaleidoscope looks like it might be a psychedelic kind a place w/these lysergic, swirling light shows, strobe lights an mirrored ceiling an they put a lot a bands on. tonight it looks like they must be throwin a Mod night or sum thing cuz there's like 7 or 8 Vespas an Lambrettas w/shit loads a mirrors stickin out all over them parked on the pavement outside. place is always full a kids smashed on Tennent's Extra, or standin about sucking on cans a Breaker lager. i tell Tripod an Hawkeye sure, sure i got sum thing for them an i go down to the door an sell them a couple a Frogs. Hawkeye's head his too small for the rest of him an he looks at me w/his one good eye, smiling inanely like a ghoul in sum circus sideshow as his bad eye goes off on its diaganol trajectory reflecting the yeller streetlight.

    they're really just a pair of total horror kids, Tripod got his name cuz he fell off sum scaffolding an now he limps about permanently on a crutch. it's like fuckin hell the both of them should be in sum kinda remake of that Freaks film an not only that i suspect these 2 might be a couple a gay bender homo faggots an they just don't even know it themselves yet. but i dunno, man, they're alright, just a couple a shitlords always jacked up on sumthin, out there lookin for sum kind a satisfaction in life they ain't never gonna find.

    always seems to be pissin down an it's the aftermath of a rainstorm again an the water is still cascading down the gutters an gushing down the drains like a black river an i'm standing here w/these 2 scrubbers in sum surreal scene.

while i'm downstairs i run a few doors along to the Hill Street Chip Bar an buy myself sum chicken an chips. there's a taxi office above the chip shop that has no public entrance, so you have to shout up to the woman who works there for a taxi. there's a group a nasty drunk city boy Colmore Row types wearing gold ear-rings an dressed in grey suits an pink shirts shouting up to her as she hangs out the winnder. horrible trendies who look exactly the types who drink at TFI Friday up on the Hagley Road an places like that where they play crap like Luther Vandross an Chaka Khan an Spandau Ballet w/all that fuckin *gold always believe in your soul* bull fucking shit. there's 5 or 6 of them an every one a the bastards sprouting these shit-for-brains ponytails. fucking *ponytails.*

this world. i tell you. it's goin right down the plug-hole.

back upstairs in my gaff i get a plate for the chicken an chips an i roll a joint an lie on the sofa watching Mickey Rourke in *Angel Heart* on VHS for like about the 5$^{th}$ time.

# 11

that morning in Sutton Park it was busy. me an Electric had to be on the case with our picking, beat the rest a the bastards to the punch. perfect pale morning light, white sun just low on the horizon an a lovely dew on the ground. must a been like 6 a.m. an there was this elderly woman w/her husband out walking their dog who i overheard say, "what are all these young people doing walking about in the grass?"

her husband didn't know either. "i've no idea," he said, watching throo squinted, questioning eyes.

we dint do too bad, got a good haul. sticky mass of couple a hundred liberty caps in our bag that we never even bothered to wash or dry before we counted out 50 each an necked at about 11 a.m. an i dunno how but we ended up in sum sedate little pub absolutely spaced in the middle a the day an it must a been like pensioner discount day or sumthin becuz we were in this pub w/a load a old folk all havin their roast dinners w/quiet background jazz muzak playing.

Electric flops down on the bench seat that curls around the corner becuz he can't even walk to the bar, "my legs have gone," he laughs. so i go up an the barman is lookin at me kind a funny w/his beady eyes but even if disdainfully he serves me anyway. his name badge says Richard Spitz. i stagger back over to our table spilling the pints all over the place, laughing uncontrollably becuz i am seeing ribbons of flourescent green an pink light streaming from the chandelier an spiralling around me, sending me reeling. glasses on tables are glinting an turning into fractals, people's eyes are growing new eyes, faces all around me morph into sumthin grotesque an become cartoon gargoyles as shimmering light comin throo the winnders turns the panes a glass into Victor Moscoso paintings.

i collapse down, my face buried in Electric's shoulder i'm grabbing him by the shirt an telling him look at the chandelier, look at the fuckin chandelier an he looks an i dunno if he can see it too but whatever he can see he immediately roars with laughter an we're both crying, rolling around w/laughter until we both slip off our chairs an roll onto the floor. i'm on my knees tryna get back up, all the old boys an girls staring at us with the daggers.

"oh, here he comes," i say as the tall, skinny Richard Spitz comes weaving round the tables towards us w/quite sum vicious intent by the look on his fizzhog. grey haired old bugger on the next table leans towards her husband who's wearing a bright yellow shirt an whispers, "i think they've been on drugs, to be honest."

the barman arrives at our table an

snatches up our drinks, "i think you 2 gentlemen had better leave," he says.

"s'alright, mister dickie-bow," i say. "we were going anyway, we wouldn't stay here w/all this bunch a fuckin gargoyles." Electric an me both have fits of laughter again. Electric leans over their table an says to the old lady, "anyone ever told you, you're a really strange looking fucker?"

"OUT! NOW!" the barman screams.

the man in the bright yellow shirt wipes his mouth w/his napkin an tosses it down on the table, he stands up an says, "i'm a good mind to take you outside an give you a good hiding, you insolent little pieces of shit! don't mess w/me, son. i'm an ex Para an i can be *fucking savage* if you get me started!"

"that's you people's answer to everything, isn't it? violence." i put my hand on his shoulder an sit him back down in his chair. "*siiit* down, Lemon Popsicle," i tell him. "there'll be no fighting here today. the war's over, sunshine. that's not how we men of peace do things." Electric falls back in his chair holding his stomach with laughter, repeating over an over: "ha ha ha ha Lemon Popsicle ha ha ha ha ha Lemon Popsicle."

everybody's stopped eating, the barman slams down the drinks an grabs me by the arm. i can't feel my own body weight as he steers me forcefully towards the door, crashing into tables along the way, knocking shit everywhere. i manage to twist around an he ends up dragging me out backwards w/his arm around my neck an i'm too spackered to fight him so i allow him his moment a glory, they'll be talking about this for weeks to come in this place, how Dick Spitz single-handedly dealt w/a couple a degenerates. but i'm throwing out my legs, purposely kicking tables over as we go for maximum dramatic effect while Electric starts dancing, clapping his hands an singing Nick Lowe's *I Love the Sound of Breaking Glass.*

we're still unable to stop laughing as we stagger out the front doors an float out into the bright white winter sunlight that hits my eyes like a nuclear flash. total whiteout, man. as we leave there's a tiny frosted glass toilet winnder open at the side of the building. Electric pulls a firework out his pocket, lights it an tosses it in. a few moments later as we're walking away across the parking lot there's a huge amplified bang from inside the pub. we almost piss ourselves laughing.

we saunter happily into Sutton Coldfield town centre but everywhere we go they take 1 look an won't serve us, not even at the Station pub, an after the firework stunt we reckon by now the blue bottles are most likely gunna be looking for us so we grab a black cab an head off back to my flat.

we spend the rest a the day sittin listenin to

Pink Floyd w/eyes closed havin sum closed eye visuals an at 6 p.m. we neck the rest of the shrooms an head into town.

* * *

there's nuthin cryptic about death. at Superfast's wake that his parents held at the Market Tavern on Moseley Street w/Electric an Amy. i don't even know what Amy's doing here. it's not like she ever gave a fuck about him. there were few tears shed at all as a matter a fact. Superfast's freaky mother who by the way looked like Alice fuckin Cooper told me, somewhat matter-of-factly i thought: "they took him to hospital an he lasted the night but a few minutes after 11 next morning he was pronounced dead. the nurse removed the tubes from his body an they wheeled him down to the cold room. an that was that. he was gone from us."

in the toilets Electric is cookin up sum speed with a Zippo an a spoon. he draws the mixture up into the syringe throo a tiny piece a sponge that he had in his coat pocket. he shoots up in his arm an within seconds his eyes are lit up like a pinball machine as if sum thing that's usually lacking in his very being has been restored to full pelt. when you're only an occasional joy-banger shooting up is like being born again, you feel this quiver of apprehension like you're not sure you wanna do it but you know you gotta do it an you know there's no turning back. it's right here, right now.

Electric passes me the rig an i shoot up while he waits for me. as the chill of the fluid flows into my arm an i get that beautiful sinking feeling in my chest like i'm dying in a fantasy he's talkin about sumthin or other but i don't have a clue what he's rattling on about but when i'm done i slap him on the back an joke: "let's get the fuck out a dodge, let's go an sniff sum glue!"

worst thing was Superfast's big, fat sister Marsha was there. i didn't even know he had a sister until now an it was terrible cuz she's got a club foot an she's in an electric wheelchair not cuz a the club foot but cuz she's just too fat to walk an she got sum kind a mental fuck-up goin on in her brain an she don't talk right at all, she does nuthin but sit in her chair stuffing herself w/food. she just communicates via a series of hand gestures, accompanied by gutteral inhuman noises that emenate deep in the back of her throat that resemble what i can only describe as being akin to cross between a turkey an a chimpanzee, or sum strange animal voice you'd hear in a jungle like this strangulated *wu-wu-wu-u-u-u-ak-ak-ak-aaargh* an it's like being stuck in *The Twilight Zone*, the blud running cold in your veins an you'd just freeze in your tracks an go: what the fuck is that, man? an all i can think when i look at this monstrosity is surely this mutant shoulda been taken in a room sum where at the hospital an quietly asphyxiated at birth. there's just no point for sum people to exist. to me, in my state, she's a real bad trip inducing horror show.

it's totally unsettling. an it had nuthin to do w/being grief stricken either, cuz she ain't grief stricken, in fact Marsha don't seem like she gives 2 shits an she just keeps stuffin her face w/sausage rolls an ham sandwiches from the buffet. it's just her natural state of being. she's wearin a Clint Eastwood tshirt w/him pointin his .44 Magnum an it says *go ahead punk, make my day.* Over that she's wearin a black bomber jacket w/Shakin fuckin Stevens on the back. an she's an evil lookin piece a work an all w/this awful shaved head, she's like no woman i ever saw w/truly malevolent staring face like Carl Panzram an she whisks about at like 100 miles an hour in her huge elctric wheelchair that's like just about the size of a fuckin Land Rover, crashing into all the chairs an tables an if you don't shift out the way quick she'll just ram into you an break your ankles w/the fuckin thing.

in any case, it was terrible cuz i wound up stuck at a table w/her an i just didn't know how to reply to the indescribable sounds that come out her mouth so i ended up just sittin there w/my bad social skills, nodding an going, "yeah,

yeah, spot on, Marsha i know what you mean." an a course everyone present knew i hadn't got a clue what she was sayin cuz no fucker else did either. totally awkward social situation to be in.

    it's dark now an there's an array a brilliant stars above us that are undeniably beautiful an beneath these stars the cocktail a drugs hits me like a tempest, i've reached that point of ego-death but i know deep inside we're all at the mercy of time. right at this moment we are all still young but youth is a vacuous beauty an since i have always found it difficult to live in my own skin i find now that i understand Superfast in that his death was a kind a suicide. there's very little evidence of my life. there are no photographs or anything like that. only photo i ever saw was one of me w/my birth father, in a park or sum where an i look about 2 years old, i'm peddling a little orange toy tractor an my dad is wearin a black suit looking down smiling at me. i don't know what happened to the photograph, sum body showed it me once an i never saw it again. my dad looked just about like i do now minus the eye-liner an torn jeans. he had the same colour a jet black hair that i do.

    Superfast must a known death was coming, actively pursued it becuz there's no escape from the constant feelings of isolation, the world around us is in a state of perpetual motion, an yet there's a complete sense of disconnection. but i know that the human race as a whole will survive, it's almost indestructible, like bacteria that will multiply an spread, it's like sum pursuing evil in a nightmare that just can't be killed. but Superfast bin lookin like a walkin corpse for last couple a years, man.

it's Friday night an the 3 of us leave the wake an bomb a gram a speed each an head for the Hummingbird. when we walk in it's still only like 11pm an everyone is already lying spackered all over the floor, out their faces on acid or whatever their drug of choice is, you gotta step over them all to get to the bar an the dancemix of the Paris Angels' *Perfume* is cascading across the delerious dancefloor in rolling waves of sound, nobody's mind extending beyond the trivial absurdities of this shared microcosmic universe.

derz a good-looking black bird w/long dredds down to her waist serving behind the downstairs bar an while i'm waitin to be served Electric sez in my ear what he always sez when he sees a black bird, he screws up his face all lascivious an goes: "still pink on the inside ain't she, eh? pink on the inside."

after getting a shot a whisky i go for a wander around the massive club. on the balcony overlooking the dancefloor i run into this tall blonde-wigged tranny i know who's called Robin or Robert or somethin but whilst in her cartoon-like female incarnation, which appears to be any other time than when she's not workin her job at Barclays Bank, calls herself Orgazma DeCock. Orgazma DeCock's wearin a glittering silver sequined dress an is holding a bright blue cocktail w/an umbrella stickin out the top in one hand an in the other has a cigarette cocked delicately in a long silver cigarette holder. she looks like she's in sum Detroit 60's girl group. in these great superhigh fuck-me pumps she has on her feet she must be nearly 7 foot tall. she comes over an slides a surprisingly gentle arm around my shoulder seductively an asks if i'm carrying her favourite. she smiles an tells me she just wants "one serving."

i like Orgazma so i sell her a Purple Ohm for the friend price of 5 quid. she drops the acid tab there an then, takes it down w/her cocktail, suckin from the straw an she hangs around for a while, smiling an blowing cigarette smoke, talkin bout nuthin much. but the speed's working its way into my system an i blurt out a nowhere i'm forming a band called the Whores of Kunt. "cunt w/a K," i impress upon her. Orgazma laughs outrageously, "you're a riot," she says, fluttering her big fake eye-lashes. an she slaps me on the arm an makes me promise i'll let her be the singer an i'm like, "yeah yeah, quite truthfully in fact you were totally the very person i had in mind."

we walk back down the stairs together, she

clomps down on her great big heels an then she draws a loud, dramtic breath an screams, "i love this song." an she flies off an just hits the dancefloor, throwing herself around, slam-dancing wrecklessly, i mean she's dancin like a bastard, barrelling onto the floor like a bowling ball, knocking everyone out the way like skittles as the DJ blasts out Jesus Jones' *Info Freako.*

    i go to the bar an get another couple a drinks an when i return to Amy an Electric she smiles spitefully an asks whose perfume it is i stink of, i point across the club at the big blonde wig an deflect her implication, "that big tranny over there." it appears to assuage her for the time being but i know that should she just fancy a fight for the sake of it at some later point in time she'll keep it in her arsenal an use it against me in sum twisted version of reality. she looks at me w/her blank face. i just pass Amy her drink an smile an say, "here, drink that an shuddup you little fuckin slut."

    Amy just stands there totally unperturbed by anythin or maybe just oblivious but in any case she's just got her usual air of defiance about her, dancing on the spot in her super short gold dress, drinking her drink an throwing her long red hair about.

    Electric's fastened himself on to some pretty, pink-haired punk bird who i recognise cuz she's Vix, who was the singer of girl pop-punk band We've Got a Fuzzbox & We're Gonna Use It. the band split up like last year in 1990 but i remember who she is. she's lookin about 50ft tall in these platform boots like sumthin outta KISS an i am amazed cuz you never see Electric talkin to women. he doesn't even fuckin know any women. he never pulls any women an i always think it's cuz he's got a slow an lethargic body shaped like a tuna fish, an his thinning greasy hair an mustache don't help one bit. but as they say even a blind squirrel occasionally finds a nut, though i don't even think he knows this girl is one a the in-crowd. an she's lookin at him all funny cuz he's just a little shitlord talkin sum absolute crap about your teeth, an i quite clearly hear the mental bastard sayin what about if y'teef were naturally flaccid an only got hard when you wanted summat to eat?

this one time Electric told me this weird story about sum bird he reckons he met a while ago an i went "yeah, really?" w/a piss-taking sneer on my lips an he sed vigorously tryna convince me, "yeah, yeah me an her we talk on the phone all the time, man." so i looks at him kind a disbelief in my eyes an sed: "yeah, what does she say?" an i put a pretend handset to my ear an go, "oh baby i'm so horny... hurry up an enter your credit card details." an Electric got all nasty an eyeballed me showin his teeth like fuckin Jaws w/his head cocked to one side an sed, "fuck off, Costine, you're not exactly CasafuckinNova yourself."

tho in any case, i take the credit for this development in his personal evolution this evening cuz the speed i gave him has temporarily loaned him a bit a zest an got him totally amped up an his mouth is flapping like a shed door in the wind even if he is talking total crap. still, Vix is probably gonna walk away in a minute. i dunno what story he's telling himself but he's yapping away all oblivious an after a while sum bald bastard, spot lights shining on his scalp, who thinks he's hot shit comes over an muslces in an goes: "hey, leave her alone, buddy. can't you see she don't wanna talk to you?" looks like his hair has retracted into his head an come back out his ears. disgusting. he looks like a cross between a mongoose an a vulture. Electric gives him the finger, looks him dead in the eye an says: "fuck you, Kojak, mind your own business." an the bald mongoose/vulture hybrid stutters about on his feet for a couple a seconds not a clue what to do next an Electric's just eyeballing this kid an it's clear the amphets have deceived his usual cowardly nature an at this point i'm thinkin oh Jesus, Electric's gonna twat this bald bastard one an then us an this kid's 3 cronies all gonna have a big scrap but after dithering about nervously the kid turns an the 4 of them just walk away. an i gotta admit i damn well feel pretty proud of Electric cuz there's nuthin i hate more than such would-be knights in shining armour tryna impress sum girl. an best thing about it is Vix puts her hand on Electric's shoulder an actually laughs at the Kojak jibe.

as Kojak walks away w/his tail between his legs Electric's enjoying the taste of victory an shouts after him, "watch yer back when you're walkin home, pussy. i'll be waitin in the shadders for yer!"

on the walk home w/Amy we're both still totally wired, both of us got eyeballs the size a the city an we scuttle cross the street to Days of the Raj Indian restaurant. there's a group of Indian men sittin at a table in the winnder eyeballin us an i run up the steps to the place but when i try the door the fuckin thing's locked but the closed sign is still swinging. i laugh an turn to Amy an go, "ahhh, shit, man. they saw us comin." the Indian men inside are all laughing too, shakin their heads like there's no way you're comin in here, sunshine. we give them a feeble wave of resignation, they wave back, an we walk away an head for sum pizza joint.

# 12

sometimes i still have nightmares about the place, that care home i was in as a child. i always remember the long, cold corridors, i remember the carers as sum sorta ghosts, disembodied entities who were there but not really *there,* they always seemed so remote. but the ghosts were small miseries in comparison to the terror i felt at the building itself, its high imposing walls, the gothic stone edifices that seemed cruel, angular, the tall blackened chimneys belching black smoke to perpetually grey skies. at night there was always the sound of crying an i often wonder whatever became a those kids. in those moments i'd never felt so completely alone. place was all rebuilt a few years ago now an during the 80s it got turned into hotel accommodation an flats, but in my mind it remains as it was an i've relived being in there a thousand times since an the image of that lost, uncherished child that was once me chills me to the bone. i'm not in love w/this world at all. it will break you. in the end it breaks everyone. it's just a question of when.

you know life's bullshit gonna get you in the end. that's just elemental. thing is, you just gotta fight it as long as you can. me, at least i can say under the circumstances of my life i was the best i could be. *under the circumstances.* in all honesty i have to add that caveat, but i can honestly say i was the best i could be an i can say that with about 80% conviction. the other 20%, well... you know the schnizzle.

it's the morning burn out, the eviscerating dreams woke me up an i'm hitting baseline. the microwave goes *ding*. i'm heating up a leftover piece a pizza at 5 a.m an Amy's still in bed. she's been mooching at my place for days now, she's called in work sick, telling them it's "women's problems." Amy sez no one ever enquires further when you tell them that. a man would prob have to go into detail an have to tell them you got blud seepin out your Jap's eye or sumthin, but women can get away w/leaving it at that. but i wouldn't know, i refuse to work. i refuse to lend my time to sum thing i don't give a flying fuck about. punching my clock. fuck that for a game a soldiers.

last few days she's been here i bin seriously suspicious cuz things between Amy an me have remained unusually calm w/no getting a wild hare up her ass about sumthin from her whatsoever an she's acting all sweet an keeps tryna convince me it's cuz things have started workin between us. it's a fucking ruse, a cover for sumthin an i know it, i just don't know what it is she's hiding.

while Amy's still sleeping i'm sittin by the

winnder blazin a bit a Buddha grass that i've cut off my own cannabis plant that i'm cultivating in its terrarium an havin a coffee. i'm looking at the criss cross a wires an railways tracks running into New Street Station, the scintillating street lights, the tower blocks. i like man made things more than nature, structures of steel an glass an stone. i think the pylon more beautiful than the tree. but these are just my surrogate thoughts, i don't suppose they mean anything in the grand scheme a things. if you boil any of us right down to the bones an sinew, none of us amount to much. the parameters of life are set, man. nuthin much any of us can do about none of it. we're just hunks a bilogical material that one day dissolves back into the morass a universal protoplasm.

Amy works at sum fucking place in Harbourne in the HR department, along w/several other females. it's sum insurance call centre. just sum dumb shit place or other. so the little matriarchy that makes up the HR department are all in their early 20s an do the CV screening of all job applicants. if it's another attractive young woman they get thrown in the trash, if it's a guy over 30 he gets thrown in the trash, if it's an ugly young guy he gets thrown in the trash. the result is only older, less attractive women get hired, an good-looking younger guys, both usually w/out relevant job compatibility. so if anyone in the actual workplace has a fucking clue what they're doing it's purely accidental. Amy told me all this. she thinks it's hilarious.

Amy looks beautiful when she's sleeping. i've been on an off in this roller-coaster relationship w/her for like nearly a year now since i came back from Los Angeles but i look at her in these calm moments an i wonder if the juice just ain't worth the squeeze. no idea why i still got her in my life.

i've got Bowie's *Hunky Dory* album on the turntable an i'm staring out the winnder at the dark, wet dawn streets littered w/newspapers blowin about, empty beer bottles an cigarette packets. a brief interval before all the bullshit starts again an the sad hordes hit the streets, trudging heavily on their ways to work just like every man jack of them bin scooped up in the nets an their minds cut out of them like fish-livers an sold on the market for a penny apiece. man, the powers that be got em all just doing backflips on the carousel.

on the corner where Hill Street meets Navigation Street traffic lights alternate an the grizzle-haired wino Bazooka Joe stands in a long overcoat draped around his warped old bones playin a harmonica, 3/4's gone bottle of alley juice near his foot. i turn my own music right down so i can listen to the doleful Billie Holiday tune he's playin. it wails out like the perfect soundtrack to the dismal, hollow city all around us an the tune tells you 1 thing; it tells you it don't mean there's no love to be had in this world, it just means sum people never find any an it's a slow deth for these people. this is a city that tries to tell you don't ever dare dream big. an you're waiting for all the beautiful things that never come an most a the populace got nuthin quantifiable in life but that don't mean sum of them ain't got souls that are rich. you just try to be the best you can but you're really just living the life you've bin left  an the thing about it all is you just don't know how long it's gonna last or how it's all going to end for you but you know whatever it is there ain't no easy way out. but most people don't love w/any depth anyway, they just love what sparkles an shines.

eventually Amy rouses an gets outta bed an goes over naked to the kitchenette, flicks on the kettle. "you havin another 1 a your mad internal monologues?" she sez w/a great gaping yawn. her mad red hair is all wild like her head's on fire.

i just stare at her for a few moments an eventually say, "i like that old saying: women should be seen an not heard."

"that's children, you dickhead," she coughs as she pulls on her underwear. "*children* should be seen an not heard. not women."

i just laugh becuz i know i've triggered her an i go back to looking out the winnder at the street. they've changed the billboard across the road. the vandalised army recruitment ad is gone, now it says Terminator 2 is on at cinemas. on the poster the model 101 T-800 is sitting on a Harley-Davidson holding a sawed off shotgun.

the teevee is on as usual w/the sound off an the sickish, grey countenance of just about the worst prime minister we've ever had, John Major is on sum news show, droning away like an old, broken propshaft. Amy stands just staring at the screen, not thinking anything, just staring for no real reason, just becuz it's there. i really got no time for these people. the purpose of the ascending political agenda is to make a virtue of your disposability. an you might even say you want a revolution but it's never what people say that matters. you say you want a revolution but you just carry on falling in line.

"government is just a puppet show," i tell Amy. "an if you look close enough you can see the strings. but what we never get to see is the puppet masters."

an you think about it, man. we're here just 1 planet amongst our little galaxy a stars an you can look up an think there's so many, so many you can't even count them. but between each of these explosions of light there's nuthin. just blackness. there's more blackness than there is stars an the truth is we don't understand none of it an we weren't meant to understand it either becuz i'll tell you this much: if mankind understood the universe we'd destroy it. we'd destroy the whole goddamn lot of it. if man knew how it all worked there'd be nuthin fuckin left.

an i roll another joint an toke on it becuz i just don't wanna think about it all anymore.

# 13

Christmas is like 4 weeks away an i'm all square w/Slant Eye an stocked up w/gear again ready to rock n roll. last night Electric an me were banging back bottles a Grolsch w/whisky chasers upstairs at the West End Bar on Rockabilly night an the DJ slamming out stuff like the Polecats, Meteors, Cramps an Stray Cats before we were back up the Hummingbird seeing the Ramones. i got so mongoled out of it on pills i barely remember a thing apart from sum how we ended up on the balcony in the guest enclosure right above the band w/these so called VIPs who were all unknown to me but no doubt sum people i should a recognised, probably sum bodies stupidly famous like Led Zeppelin or sum fucking body but i hadn't got a clue. at sum point sum stupid cunt right below us on the dancefloor managed to climb up like twenny foot or sum thing an was dancing on top a stack of like 10 Marshalls at the side a the stage an fell off an they had to stop the show for about 5 mins while security carried him off either unconscious or dead, i dunno which.

after the show we just hung about in the deserted club while the roadies were clearin shit away an the barstaff swept up all the discarded plastic beer glasses. Electric an me were just talkin bout sumthin an nuthin when Joey Ramone ambled out a the back an Electric shouted him an he comes over an sed sum stuff to us that i don't even remember before handin me a drum skin signed by the whole band an walkin away back stage. he also turned to Electric an sed, "hey, you need this, man" an gave him this kind a square, flat ballpoint pen that on one side it said **DRUGS DESTROY** w/some helpline telephone number on it an on the other side Joey signed it himself w/black marker pen an Joey Ramone laughed an sed, "be sure to call that number, man" an then he laughed an walked away.

musta come out the Ramones gig bout midnight absolutely shitfaced an for sum reason that is completely unknown to me we ended up like fishes outta water in Tressine's nightclub where i was carryin this drum skin about w/me an we both bombed down another acid tab an got totally strung out. Tressine's is kind a like sum shimmering trendy place on Newhall Street just off Colmore Row, all the girls in tawdry cocktail dresses an the men in chinos an tossed sweaters, the lights in the place were all kitsch pink an gold an the music was all Madonna an Taylor Dayne an Luther Vandross an a whole swathe a shit like that, bit a Duran Duran thrown in. whole place was just a pleb's vision of glamour an the wooden people in there who got low level jobs in banks an shit like that were all blonde hair an fake sun tans, all thinking they're hot shit an i look around an i mean this place is like we got on a coach trip to shit town an it's like 5 quid in on the door an it's only a quid a pint so everyone is totally fuckin shitfaced. sum kid w/pineapple hair sprouting out his head that looked terrible like Howard Jones wanted to look at the Remo drum skin an then goes, "oh shit you got it signed, too. you wanna hold onto that."

i can only piece fragments of the night together but i got this putrid memory of like garish gold curtains around the dj's box an the dj was this 5ft tall peroxide blonde freak ass man w/narrow shoulders an a big chickenshit bouffant hair-do who looked like David Van Day outta that shit 80's pop duo Dollar stuck in my head. not only that but when he came out of his box to get an orange juice from the bar it looked like he'd got a great big lobster or sum thing stuffed down the front of his pants an there's me thinkin oh Christ that'll do it, Amy'll be transfixed an probably fuck off home w/him at the end a the night. plus the fact is she does that kind a shit, fucking other guys, just to get at me. of course, i rise above it. i do not react to her bullshit.

i got the signed Ramones drum skin hangin on a nail on my wall. but just below that, sitting on the bookcase, my eyes drift down to the empty terrarium an i only just realise now that Amy's nicked my fucking cannabis plant. it's gone, the whole thing ripped out the compost by its roots. i go over joylessly an switch the now pointless Philips grow-lamp off.

an then, not only that, but when i walk into the bedroom i find that the mad bitch has cut up my leather trousers an my vintage 1960's MC5 tshirt an thrown the hundreds a fragments all over the bed. another freak out. an i got absolutely no idea why.

# 14

before walking round to Edwards No' 8 metal club on Lower Severn Street just around the block from my gaff tonight i watched this porn film starring Christy Canyon. there was this scene in a messy kind a warehouse office w/an IBM computer on the desk w/green monitor going blip blip blip about sum thing or other an carboard boxes stacked up everywhere so maybe it was a shipping clerk's office, sum thing like that but in any case she was w/this skinny young kid, man, he looked about 15 or 16, little more than a boy an she was pretending to enjoy it, puttin in the great performance like Christy always does, but i mean for fucksake this skinny kid got the smallest cock i've ever seen. i didn't even know it was possible for a man to have a cock that small. but she let him cum in her mouth, his cock so small she could get the whole thing in balls deep no problem at all an even w/a full fuckin hard-on this bastard wouldn't even have touched her tonsils, man. so i dunno how the fuck he got a job performing in the porno industry. Christy was young in this film though, i think it was like 1985 an i know she was born in '66, one year older than me, so in this flick she'd a been like 19 an she looked absolutely great. but i've no idea who the kid was, i imagine he didn't get much work in the industry an went off to work on a factory production line or sum thing. or maybe he made a bit a dough tryna peddle his own line of penis enlargement pills, i dunno.

\* \* \*

i'm in Eddy's w/my blonde an beautiful ex girlfriend Samantha who's back down from Sheffield Uni where she's studying literature or media or sum thing, maybe both. she's like 22 now an i ain't seen her for nearly 2 years but she rang me up last night an said she was on a flying visit to see her parents an did i wanna hook up for a couple of hours an i'm like yeah sure. i'm wearing a pair of battered old 501's w/the Boys Brigade belt an now i can't believe it never occured to me at the time but when she sees me Sam stares at it amused, open mouthed an tells me it telegraphs a totally gay message. she laughs an goes: "may as well just wear a tshirt that says 'i'm queer.'"

we're on the top floor a the club an they're playing Morbid Angel an Slayer an all that stuff that's alright but neither of us are totally into but it's better up here than w/those people on the other floors an the death-metal kids are wreckin the dancefloor in a swirl a smoke an lights. on the way in the bouncers stopped me again but this time really did only pull out a bona fide packet a Tic Tac mints out my pocket so they let me in. i've hit on a good stratagem an make a mental note: always carry a real packet a mints in future, it distracts them. bout 15 mins later i ran into a group of 5 stupid Canadian exchange student kids hanging round the bar who seemed like they'd believe you knew the Queen if you told them you did. so i sold 1 of them them 4 wraps of crushed up Tic Tacs that i mixed in w/a tiny bit of Ajax powder that the cleaners obviously left lying about in 1 a the toilet cubicles to lend it a bona fide acerbic taste for the special price of thirty quid, knowin i'd be long gone before they suspected sumthin.

Eddy's is on 3 floors. on the bottom floor it's like where all the wizened old mutants sit cuz it's all prog rock, trad rock an American fm rock. you get a bit a not bad stuff like Rush, ELO, Hawkwind, Pink Floyd but it's mixed in w/crap like REO Speedwagon, Chicago an a special kind a crap like Toto, blessin the fuckin rains down in Africa an all that sorta malarky. you can sell those fuckers downstairs a bit of acid sum times, especially the Grateful Dead crowd tryin to resurrect the lost 60s drop-out dream. but overall it's like an old people's home down there.

on the middle floor in Eddy's is where they play stuff like AC/DC, Def Leppard, Iron Maiden an you can't usually sell those beer-bellied pricks anythin at all, they're all just fat 10 pints a night pissheads. an their cheap sidekicks who're into all the 80s hair metal scene like Motley Crue an L.A. Guns are just like stevie-boy lager-lad thugs in drag, they got silky scarves all hangin of them an shit like that. i mean i like a lot a that music just fine but on the top floor where Sam an me are sittin now is where they play all the heavy stuff an the goth-rock kids up here will take almost anything but are usually happy w/a gram or 2 of white lightning cuz despite popular belief they ain't miserable, they're a pretty gregarious crowd a kids when amongst their own kind. one thing i noticed tho is you never see a pregnant goth girl. think about it, you ever seen a pregnant goth? no, you haven't. you see em w/kids but never actually pregnant. an i've come to the conclusion it's cuz goth girls don't give birth, they lay eggs in their beds an wait for them to hatch before the little gothlings are brought out into the light of day. it's a different species altogether. i'm tellin you, you don't even wanna start thinkin about the breeding practices of the goth. different world.

    Samantha an me are sittin huddled at a table up the corner. i drop a couple of 30mg codeine tablets just becuz i like the slight feeling of numbness it gives you w/out being totally out of it an Sam just takes a sip of her drink an sniffs at me w/her nose held just slightly up in the air an says ruminatively: "you shouldn't do things like that, Mark." an we're talking about the past. her blonde waist length hair is wild an glossy an shining an she just looks like a young Brigitte Bardot in her little short leather skirt an black stockings. an she tells me she thought by now i'd have facilitated my own demise. "i thought you'd have hurtled over the edge by now," she says. "i honestly thought you'd be dead." an she tells me how she thought i was a maniac an if she stayed in my life i'd have taken her over the cliff w/me. so i just look at her an say, "hey, would you like a kiss?" Sam's finger nails are painted alternately silver an black.

the truth is in a way i am terrified of her, it's like lookin into the eyes of a beautiful but deadly predator but i think that's maybe down to my own experiecnes cuz she's just about the sanest girl i ever knew. an she smiles an says, "i suppose i wouldn't mind a kiss." an i cup her face in my palm an say, "Sam, look at me. i know i'm a dickhead but i always loved you. an i still do. i'm crazy about you." an her eyes soften an they're the most beautiful green eyes i've ever seen an she smells of sum sweet perfume an we kiss an right in that moment it seems like it's the most beautiful thing i've ever felt deep inside me. an then she sez, "you might be a dickhead but you are beautiful, i mean you're really beautiful an i wanted to sleep w/you from the moment i saw you again tonight. that intense sexual thing between us... it's still there, Mark. there's sum thing intensely sexual about you an i don't know what it is."

"you want another drink?" i say.

"nah," she kisses me again. "let's go back to your place. but you know i've got a boyfriend back up in Sheffield, right? i love him an i'm only here w/you becuz i know i've got a good fuck at the end of the night an there's no way he's gonna find out."

i try to conceal the little stabbing sensation

inside my chest becuz the truth is i want Sam to like me, to like me as a person, an i just shrug an go "yeah whatever" an i start to put my leather jacket on for us to leave an just as i've got my arms stuck in the jacket i see her comin at me out a no where like a bullet, man.

    i dunno where the hell she come from. its Amy an i'm thinking oh Christ i need this right now like i need a shotgun blast to the face. an she comes barrelling over shouting the usual "right, you bastard!" an totally kicks over the table sending empty glasses crashing everywhere an she throws a pint in my face an she's screaming i don't know what an the drink's in my eyes an i can't properly see the cuffs an slaps around my head comin in an i'm trying to get out the way but to make matters worse the bouncer wades over an grabs hold a me an i'm wearing a *Star Wars* tshirt an the smartass goes, "c'mon, Obi-Wino Kenobi, let's go!" Amy eggs him on, screaming: "yeah, get the little cunt out." an despite me trying to tell him i ain't done nuthin the chickenshit retarded goon tries to get me round the neck an drag me out backwards but i twist round an i fumble around blind an grab a pint glass from sum table an i smash it across his face in one sweeping roundhouse movement that he just don't see comin at all an i follow it up w/an immediate headbutt, he goes down like a sack a fuckin shit w/the blud pouring from the side of his head but he scrambles back up, his blonde flat-top hairdo like he thinks he's Ivan Drago out a *Rocky* turned red w/his own blud an now the other 2 gorrilas sprinted over an are on me.

the house lights have all come on bright like floodlights but the DJ ain't killed the decks an we're brawling to a soundtrack of Megadeth's *Killing Is My Business* an the goons are dragging me out the door, i manage to elbow one of them in face hard but they get me in a chickenshit choke-hold an drag me out an half throw me down the narrow staircase an then the 3 of them are on me again laying in knees to my ribs, punching me in the side a the head but i mean i'm toked up to the fuckin hilt an i can't feel a fuckin thing an i'm going, "i'll kill the fuckin lot of yer." an they get a hold a me by the arms they're tryna drag me out the fire escape into the street but every time they get me far as the door i throw my legs up an get my foot on the door frame, pushing us back. i get another elbow to one a their faces as we all go down backwards an hit the deck in a mauling embrace before they finally pick me up an ram me against the wall, taking the breath out a me. 2 of them get hold a me an throw me onto the pavement outside an slam the door. 30 seconds later the door opens briefly an Sam calmly steps out an i mean she just stands an puts this open-mouthed incredulous look on me, hands on her hips an says, "Jesus Christ, Mark. you don't change do you?"

i get to my feet, spit out blud. an she puts her arm in mine an says, "c'mon let's go."

we walk around the block to my gaff, Sam looks at all the blud down the front a my leather jacket an she kinda laughs at me an strokes my face gently an sez, "are you ok?"

an i tell her sarcastically, "yeah yeah, don't worry you'll still get your fuck later."

"don't be a dick. i'm serious," she says. "i mean are you going to be alright? you're pretty banged up."

"yeah i'm just a bit bruised about the ribs. but that's the goon's blud, not mine," i say. i'm feeling totally embarrassed, in truth becuz i want her to think sumthin of me, i don't want her to think i'm just sum fuckin loser.

there's a full moon in the sky, beautiful an dazzling silver above John Bright Street as we walk arm in arm round to my gaff. on the corner there's sum mutant skinny to fuck wino dressed as Santa w/his rolled-up sleeping bag on his back an little begging cap on the pavement. the Santa suit is hanging off his skinny frame an he's not even playin any instrument or singing or nuthin, he's just desperately jigging about to a ghettoblaster playin Slade's totally piss poor *Merry Christmas Everybody*. now that's a song i hate.

we walk past him an it's just such a depressing sight you can't help but feel a stab of anguish right in your gut for the man so i at least just chuck a quid in his cap an as we walk on by Sam says tersely but w/her disarming smile, "so, who's that girl?"

i look her right in the eyes an shrug an say, "the kind a girl you'll burn your heart out trying to please."

"she seems a bit of a wild cat?" Sam says, angling for more. "i'm more of a domesticated cat, myself," she laughs.

"she's nuthin to me." i say diffidently as i possibly can. an i'm telling the truth, in fact. Sam just pulls a funny face i can't truly read, looks at the floor, looks a little disappointed about sum thing or other. but i dunno, i'll never know how any of these women's minds work. it's all an enigma to me. Sam's walking along beside me, her shoulder bumping against me as she walks an she's being all quiet an seemingly decorous but i can see her mind mulling tonight over an whatever she's thinking about me it obviously ain't gonna be sumthin good.

i light a cigarette. "you should stop smoking, too," Sam says. "it's not good for you."

i study the Marly between my fingers intensely. i look up at the stars. "i like to smoke," i tell her. "it gives me sumthin to do."

i don't quite feel like going home just yet after all that shit, i need to simmer down, so i walk Sam couple a blocks further down to the

Sunset Cinema Club on Hinckley Street an it's funny becuz Sam's like really middle class an she's still young an a little bit sheltered so far in life an she comes from this like toffee nosed area of Solihull an she stops dead in her tracks an stares at the seedy lookin joint that's on a dark, unlit corner in these back streets an she's holding onto my arm an she laughs an says, "holy shit, Mark. you takin me in there? i've never been to a porno place before!" she's a little bit excited to experience sumthin that's new to her an always is epecially delighted if it's sumthin that seems transgressive to her present understanding of things. in short, she's young an adventurous an up for anything, like girls such as her always are.

    we get popcorn an couple a cans a Coke at the foyer an walk in half-way throo the film an there's about 4 lone mutants in there sittin miles apart from each other. it's dark an shadowy an we take some seats near the back away from the others an we plonk ourselves down an Sam shakes her head laughing an goes, "i can't believe you've brought me in here." an i just look at her an say, "i know all the class joints."

    it's a German film from the 70's w/subtitles starring Patricia Rhomberg. the film is set in a court room but becuz we missed the beginning i'm not sure what the court case is about but the whole thing has turned into a massive orgy w/everybody fucking all over the place an the scene is goin on for ages w/the focus of the cameras shifting from participant to participant but the main focus of action it keeps returning to is the principle judge guy railing Patricia from behind as she's tossing her long brown hair about, bending her over his desk before finally turning her over onto her back an cumming all over her hairy pussy an as she grinds herself against his cock the credits start to roll an a blasting loud rendition of the German national anthem plays us out.

\* \* \*

back at my place afterwards Sam is just a beautiful bright blonde vision ambling about my place checking out the contents of my book case an briefly flipping throo my vinyl as i put a bottle a wine in the ice-bucket an put the Cult's *Dreamtime* lp on the turntable. an i can't take my eyes off her an i know that she's beautiful an feminine an there is sum thing unexplainable but real between us an it feels so immediately like she's never been away at all. an i look at her an i know she is made to be adored, not necessarily understood an i would marry this woman tomorrow if i could. we lie down on the bed w/our drinks an i rest up on one elbow an slide my hand inside her top an caress her firm breasts, her nipples are hard an she's breathing heavy an her mouth is hot an she don't have to say nuthin, i can sense every inch of her body an fibre of her being wants to fuck me.

i've undone her top an we're just playin around an i mean i am absolutely dizzy w/desire for her, i've got a felt tip pen an i'm drawing little yellow daisies on her chest an she's lying there smiling, letting me do it, an i say: "this is just an excuse to touch you." an as i undo her clothes she laughs an goes, "you think i don't know that?"

i slide 2 fingers inside her an she arches her back pushing against me an she holds my hard cock in her cool hand going oh yes, Mark, oh yes i want you to fuck me an her dilated eyes flickering in the half-light of the room. she grabs my hair an pulls me down to kiss me, sliding her tongue into my mouth. "fuck me w/your big cock," she gasps breathlessly. in her eyes, in her eyes like 2 binary planets, i have seen the complexity of her being, i have seen the pleading for affection, i have seen the ferociously sexual, i have known the offering of love big as an ocean an her violence like a hurricane. an in that one trembling moment inside her i feel her heart beating right throo me, the blood rushing vitally throo her veins. in that moment she is a part of me an i fall into her oceanic green eyes an she's writhing beneath me, i'm fucking her hard an biting her shoulders an her breasts an she holds me tight an says, "i love it when you bite me an shit... oh god i'm coming, i'm coming. Mark, i'm gonna come all over you.... all over you."

* * *

the intoxicating physical sensations of being w/Sam make me feel human once more. but now the following cold morning after she's gone again her lipstick stain left on the wine glass sitting on the table next to the bed compounds my sense of lonliness. i feel utterly alone an empty, like i didn't even know i was alone before but now i become abruptly aware of the fact an i realize that she don't even know anything about how she leaves me floundering in her wake like this, w/this complete sense of abandonment. an as i'm washing the wine glasses in the sink i stop an stare at her lipstick stain an i am overwhelmed w/this total sense of heaviness inside me an i cannot even recalibrate myself an i know that she thinks i'm just sum insensitive prick an probably don't even think i am capable of feeling anything like this. everything seems lost, damaged an desolate. i'm all broken up inside w/this total sense of desolation that i can't even charaterize an yet i know it's not her fault. it's not her fault, it's just sumthin that's buried deep inside me that she awakens an it comes up an breaks out my skin.

# 15

whole area is all demolished an rebuilt into sumthin else now. but i'm sitting on 1 a the benches down Manzoni Gardens in the middle a St. Martin's Circus in the shadder of the Rotunda near the decrepit queer's toilets down there, known as the Cottages. i'm waitin for Electric before we head off to a gig. the queers drift in an outta the toilets all day. there's globs a sum kind a glue-like substance dripping from the ceiling an there's glory holes carved in all the partitions an you don't go in there unless you're lookin for sumthin. i really had to go in for a piss once, sum kid looked no more than 16 comes next to me an pulls out his hard-on, stood lookin expectantly at me, waitin for me to do sumthin but i just finished my piss an looked at him blank an walked out, cool as a cucumber. no fuckin sweat, man.

i tell you, even the religious mutants don't even bother comin down here tryna save any body's soul. sum times the frequenters get more than they bargained for; i know sum body dint wanna pay for his blowjob an got his throat cut for all his chutzpah. rightly so, too. cheating cunt.

there's this 1 rentboy hangs around the Cottages known as Footjob who was born fucked up. got his hands where his feet should be an his feet where his hands should be. gets about w/all his legs trussed up in this special walking apparatus. poor bastard. but there's clearly plenty a freaks who convene in the joint who love that kind a stuff. Footjob plies his trade down there an you gotta feel sorry for him but the twat probably makes more money than me, or you. or even both of us put together.

while i'm waitin on the bench this slim little twink in thick blue eye-shadder comes out the Cottages an comes over an sits down next to me, he's wearin a little polka dot silky shirt tied in a knot at the waist showing his tanned flat stomach an a pair a 501's an he's got hair like Billy Idol. he crashes me a cigarette, shakes his head wildly an says, "bad night, kid."

the sun is going down an a beautiful shade a gold is permeating Manzoni Gardens, the familiar hiss a the traffic going all around us seems tranquil an calming until the abrupt shriek of a police siren shatters the ambience.

"no good?" i ask him, sparking us both up w/the old Zippo.

"made a measly fuckin fiver, bout you?" he says blowin 2 tendrils a smoke in the air out the corners of his mouth.

"oh, i'm just waiting for a friend."

"straight?"

"me? yeah."

"you're alright," the twink says. "wish i was."

"you don't like being queer?"

"nah, spose i like being queer just fine." he gestures towards the Cottages, "it's just... all this, you know. it's difficult sum times. a difficult life, you know?"

"yeah, sure."

man, he's a good-looking kid, you'd look at him walking down the street an think he was a model. i guess he's about 19. sum times you have to wonder how it all goes for people. he's like me, like any of us, just playin w/the cards he got dealt. never get on your high-horse, man. we're all just hustling throo life best we can an people gotta stop killin each other for no good reason.

i see Electric coming towards us an i tell the twink thanks for the ciggy, i gotta shoot. "i hope business picks up for you, man," i say, an i get up an walk away.

"who's that?" Electric asks w/a frown, jerking his head back towards the benches. "you havin your first homosexual experience?" he laughs.

"don't be a cunt all your life," i shrug as we head off. "just sum kid who was talkin to me."

an that was that. we go on our way an i never see the twink again. to this day i often remember that brief moment an wonder what became of him, what twists an turns his life might a took. at this point we are all so young an beautiful in our own unique ways – before the world kills your soul. but truth is we're all too young to even know it. the wisdom to appreciate it comes too late.

so we're gonna see this band. Christmas come an went while i was banged up inside. it's March 1992 an it's the first gig since i got out an the first 1 a the year for me, The Action Swingers at JB's club just off junction 10 a the M6.

yeah, fuzz come round my gaff late the following afternoon an arrested me for the glass attack on the goon. the 2 plain clothes cops come in my gaff an one of em pulls out his badge an he obviously didn't think i was paying due attention or like i didn't understand the gravity of the situation so he says forcefully: "do you see *that*?" an i goes, "yeah. so what is it? bob-a-job week?" an after that one he grabs hold a me by the neck an they cuff me up an haul me outside to their car. judge give me 6 months in Featherstone prison, Wolverhampton. but i'm out now after doing only 3.

before my court appearance Slant Eye took me out an got me into a black suit an he took me an got sum haidresser to cut all my hair short an now i still look like sum clean-cut college kid an though i'm back in my slacker clothes i still don't feel like myself at all. i'm like Samson out the bible, all my verve has gone along w/my hair.

it weren't too bad in there. like anyone would be, at first i was scared a gettin ass raped more than anythin else. but it didn't happen to me. i was sharing a room w/this blonde-haired kid called Lizard who'd got these unnerving boggle eyes an was from Newcastle who'd been in an out a prison most of his adult life. Lizard was in this time for goin around robbing vending machines. the kid licked his lips a lot w/his little nervous darting tongue that flicked out like he was lookin for a insect to eat. he licked his lips an told me, "keep your head down an don't try an come the hard-knock an you'll be alright. don't go around tryna make friends w/anyone but be sound if they come to you. but most of all, just keep your gob shut an don't go swaggerin about thinkin your sum kinda big shot. in the slammer, the only ones who get no respect ever are the kiddie-fiddlers. you ain't a kiddie-fiddler, so keep your bonce down an you'll be alright."

Lizard made me a weapon "just in case" which was a glove w/another smaller glove hidden inside an the one inside had metal upholestery tacks sharpened to a point an sewn in place on the knuckles. he sed, "punch em right in the fuckin throat."

they say prison gives you time to think. an i thought. i thought about it all an in the final analysis i still come to the conclusion that i don't believe in anything. there is nuthin in this world. there is the sea an there is the sky an nuthin that lies between means anything. there is life an there is death, like a pact w/the devil it's all perfectly signed an sealed the moment you are born an no snake-oil salesmen w/their religions or their politics ever saved anyone from the fact. i come to the conclusion all you can do is mechanise emotion so you don't feel pain anymore. i don't even think there's any such thing as love, there are just voids inside us that we need to fill in order to survive sum how, an when we find that fullfilment we call it love. i've come to the conclusion that humanity as a whole is just this monster, an just as in all the films in the end the monster has to perish. an eventually we will. we definitely will. we're gonna perish big style.

so as Spring is just about starting to kick in i'm back out the slammer an Electric tells me i gotta come an see this grunge kind a band from New York w/Bob Bert, former drummer w/Sonic Youth on drums play JB's. "Well, to be honest," Electric explains. "if they were from Seattle they'd get called grunge but they're from NY so they get called punk." an Electric's bought me a ticket as a comin out a nick gift so we're in Balloons Wine Bar on Ablewell Street in Walsall knocking back a few lagers w/vodka chasers before we taxi over to the gig. we been here since bout 4 p.m. so we're already pretty much totally spazzed. i don't know the band we're going to see so i ask Electric, "they any good?"

"well," he sez. "it's like going to a restautrant an you kinda know there's chicken on the menu."

i think for a long while but i just got no idea what he's on about. "i don't understand that analogy," i tell him.

"it's like this, i mean you go to a restaurant, right?"

"right."

"an don't matter where you go, you always know chicken is gonna be on the menu, yeah?"

"yeah, spose so."

"well, chicken's alright an all that but there are other more interesting things. the Action Swingers are the other things. get me?"

"yeah, but that's a strange analogy."

"you seem subdued," Electric says. we're sittin round the corner out the way up the back a the joint near the small rear bar that's all closed down.

"well... you know i gotta get back into the swing a things, know what i mean?"

"they broke your spirit, man." Electric pontificates w/a tone of reckoning that i don't like.

"they haven't broke my spirit," i assure him. "far from it." i give Electric the finger an just so he gets the message i let him watch me take a gram wrap out my pocket, twist it up in a Rizla an bomb it down w/my drink. "so, fuck you. an... fuck you again." i say.

"i'm just sayin it seems to me like your spirit's broken, that's all."

"well, it isn't." i affirm.

"it seems like it is."

"shut the fuck up, man. they haven't broke my fuckin spirit. you're like a bastard woodpecker." i flick his glass making a ding w/my fingernail an ask the shitlord if he wants another one or what? an i get up an go down to the front bar. i am pretty sure Electric sees himself as some more highly evolved being walking graciously amongst humanity, passing his judgements w/sum obliging wave of his hand.

i used to go to school with this kid Dale Dufus, pronounced *doofus* an that's for real, i'm telling you. Dale *Doofus.* my most enduring memory from school of him is that he couldn't swim. he absolutely hated the water an used to flounder around the edges of the pool holding onto the rail with one hand an w/the other holding onto this polystyrene flotation thing, presumably becuz if he let go he just sank like a rock. the teachers just left him alone, i mean they totally gave up trying to get him to swim. he was the only black kid in the class, it was predominantly a white kid's school, i mean they obviously just didn't let black kids in the joint an we only had 2 or 3 at the whole school, so i'm guessing the teachers just assumed it was probably true that black people can't swim so they just left him to splash about, a hopeless primordial case, in their eyes.

Dufus is standing at the bar with a pint a Guinness, fingering his goatee beard an smokin a cigarette. Dufus is actually super smart an he makes a good bit a money more than any teacher these days wholesaling counterfeit band tshirts an later, after we left school i did a bit a business w/him but i'm outta that game now. he don't look at me directly but when i get to the bar he smiles this big kinda complicit smile, showing his big white teeth an sez, "arrright, Cribs?" for sum reason he always jokingly called me Cribbins or Cribs for short an i never knew why. an i nod an say, "hey, Dale. how's the tshirt business?" an he looks at me out the corner of his eyes an his smile gets even bigger as he says, "*sweeeet!*"

i come back from the bar carrying the drinks an it's like Electric's been ruminating the issue further in his mind an i don't know if he's tryin hard to wind me up or what but as i sit back down he sucks his mustache in a most unsavoury manner an continues, "it's like you let them get to you. if it ain't that then it's these batshit crazy girlfriends of yours, man. i mean they're all nuts."

"in your opinion," i say. i don't even know why i'm tryin to justify myself to this little chickenshit in his garish green Hawaian shirt. an today he's got the buttons right open an he's got sum sorta gold ingot thing dangling down his chest. it's like what the fuck?

"it *is* my opinion. it's my *informed* opinion," he says curtly. there is a long pause an then he can't stop himself adding, "you don't seem the man you were... just sayin, that's all."

"you know Amy," i say. "that's about it. you don't really know any others."

"well, see. now i have it on very good authority that girl's on the fucking game."

"well, granted, in her case that would not surprise me. but here's the thing, smart-ass, i don't give a fuck about her. i don't care what she does."

"i'll tell you what she does do, she talks too much. she's always got far too much to say."

"that's alright," i counter. "i just stick my cock in her mouth. that shuts her up."

"i'm being serious, Mark. it was that bitch who grassed you up to the law, man."

"no shit, Sherlock. tell me summat i don't know, you fuckin faggot! but i been inside a couple a months, not 10 years. they ain't broke me."

"i'm just callin it as i see it in front a me right now," Electric shrugs condescendingly.

"drrrr drrrr drrrr, Jesus H. Christ," i go. "like a fuckin woodpecker drillin away. that's what i'm gonna start callin you - the woodpecker! you don't know jack-shit you fuckin Dodo."

"you ever thought about getting a job?" Electric sez suddenly, looking thoughtful an being totally serious. "i mean, like gettin a proper job? i've been thinkin about it a lot myself."

"nah," i go, taking a swig a my drink. "havin a job's boring, man. an i look around sum times an it's all goin on. you know, sum body diggin up the road, sum body up on a roof, hammering away. sum body paintin a fence. an i look an i just ask myself if all this constant work really needs to be done. an i don't think it does. all this work does not need to be done. it's a fuckin illusion."

i've got this new pair a black leather monkey boots on my feet an i'm like totally unsure about them now, i'm secretly wondering if they look like spastic boots, like those boots the fuckin doctors stick on spastics. tryin to change the subject i ask Electric, "hey, did you think anything about these boots when you saw them?"

"what like?" Electric questions back, looking down at my feet, frowning.

"well, i just wondered if anything, you know... struck you when you saw them?"

"What? like that they look like spastic shoes or sumthin?"

"yeah, exactly!"

Electric shakes his head, smiling an then

stares off across the other side a the empty bar an says, "no, i didn't think anythin like that. they're lovely boots. really smart."

he's got me. but i don't say anything.

after a long silence Electric nods towards the front bar, "who was that black bloke you were just talking to before?"

"oh that's Mikey the Fish," i tell him. "we were in the school swimming team together."

"yeah?" Electric looks over at Dufus, gives him the once over, looks down at his drink, looks back at Dufus, then back at me w/squinted eyes. "was he any good?"

"oh yeah, he sliced throo that water like *swoooosh!*." i go. "we used to call him Mikey the Fish or... *the torpedo!*"

"no shit?"

"no shit!"

\* \* \*

the speed's kicking well in an i feel like i got kerosene burnin throo my veins. my senses are shot to pieces, everythin's like 1000 miles an hour. there's like twenny people at this gig which is a shame cuz the Action Swingers are blowing the roof off the place. but at least that makes it a cinch to keep gettin to an from the bar an by the time they wrap up the gig Electric an me are fucking wrecked.

afterwards as the band are clearing their

gear away Electric an me go walkin towards the stage an Ned Hayden rollin up his mic cable nods down at my feet an goes sarcastically, "yo, nice boots, man."

the band hang around jokin about w/us for a while an Electric gives Ned the Drugs Destroy pen Joey Ramone gave him to sign sum autographs for us an Ned looks at it before he signs my autograph book an goes, "whooooa! take heed."

an i'm like pretty plastered on the drink an the white lightnin, voices an sounds are echoing in my ears, an i don't totally know what's being said but we're tellin them we're gonna see Sonic Youth in a couple a months an Bob Bert says, "do me a favour, give em a message from me." an i go, "yeah, what?"

"tell em i sed fuck the Sonic Youth," he laughs.

w/stars dim above us, muted by streetlights, i have a piss up against the wall beneath the blue lit neon Budweiser sign while we hang around outside on the carpark smokin a couple a joints an wait for a taxi to shoot 3 miles down the road into town an finish up the night in Equals, a seedy little nightclub at the back a the ABC Cinema in the Townend Bank area of Walsall.

when we walk in already buzzing the dj's playin *Sons of the Stage* by World of Twist. we used to come here a lot on a Saturday night. it was the first gaff i ever saw where they got those blue strip lights in the toilets that don't work anyway but're sposed to stop people being able to dig for a vein. that's the kind a clientele the place pulls in so i know i can make a few quid sellin couple a wraps a the old white lightnin in here no problem. i sell one to this kid called Jonesy an end up selling a couple more to a bunch a dipshit kids i never met before in the toilets who're all like madly into the Manic Street Preachers an they're askin me what i think a the punk music scene right now an i just make sum meaningless glib comment like, "yeah, it's all comin back, man" before i walk out the toilets back into the club where i find Electric standin alone at the bar, his greasy hair shining in the spotlights, his gold ingot glinting.

    i get another drink, lean w/my back against the bar an look across the pulsing dancefloor at all the girls w/their short skirts, fishnet stockings an Dr. Martens throwin their long hair about an i turn to Electric an say tersely: "i'd fuck anythin in here tonight."

Electric laughs an goes, "anythin?"

    "anythin!"


    at 3 a.m the pair of us are outside Walsall college gettin in the back of a taxi totally paralytic, w/no girls in tow. sum greasy haired hobo in a long coat comes walkin over holdin a paper cup an goes, "hey, you got any spare change?" i tell him no i ain't an he pulls out a huntin knife an sez, "i'll slit your fuckin throat, kid." an i just stare at the bedraggled creature an go, "try it. i'll take that off yer an cut yer fuckin balls off" an he just stands there blank for like twenny seconds before staggering away. Electric feelin totally emoboldened shouts after him, "get a fuckin job, you loser."

every time you walk down the street you look around you see how small an pointless an puny human existence truly is. truth is, human beings are as significant as a cigarette burn in the sun. on a universal scale none of us matter at all.

fuckin raining again. police sirens bellowing in the distance. Electric looks at me w/his maudlin bloodshot eyes an goes, "wim goin home pussyless again." an i'm like, "no shit, Sherlock," i fall across the backseat, holdin the taxi door open for him with my foot, "just get the fuck in an shut your mouth, it's *your* fault, you ugly fuckin bastard."

# 16

on the very cusp of O.D. i come to my senses pulled up by the side a the road on Heartlands Parkway. don't know why i took this route, how i got here. the radio is on an M/A/R/R/S *Pump Up the Volume* is playin. in the rear view mirror my eyes like 2 dead stones an my eye-lids turnin deathly blue an i'm weak an empty as if the marrow bin sucked out my bones.

stars fading out. dying moon. passing headlights. crimson simmers on the horizon as another day begins but perceptions are struggling to register as real information in my mind. i slam the auto-box into D an pull back on the Parkway. i make it back, careering into the city an ditch the stolen Toyota other end a Hill Street an bail out, leaving the keys in the ignition an stagger the 500 yards or what ever round to my flat. as i'm about to reach my door i run into the Olsen kid who's comin down the street an he just looks at me like he's seeing a zombie right before his eyes an he 's got this total look a shock an he goes, "shiiiiiit, Mark. what's happened to you?" an i don't even answer him i just lurch throo the derelict shop door, slam it behind me an throw up again as soon as i'm inside an Olsen's just peerin throo the dirty winnders watchin me w/these big bug eyes an a cigarette stickin out his mouth.

\* \* \*

for a week i was sick, anemic an dehydrated in bed. must a dropped in mass to sum sickeningly paltry weight like a 120lbs or sum thing deathly. couldn't eat or even keep a fuckin chickenshit glass a water down, i was just continually wretching up my stomach lining. i mean i was like a green skeleton w/big black fuckin circles round my sunken eyes, i was a ghastly image staring back in the mirror an i knew this time it was bad. i no longer knew who i was an when i looked at all my possessions dotted about my flat it was as if they belonged to another man from another time an another place. sounds of the city resounding starkly in my skull. i looked outside an i felt displaced from the world around me an the city had a sense of hollowness about it, like the wind blowing throo a rusty tin drum an the street lights comin throo the winnder cast my shadder on the opposite wall an it seemed to me like the twisted shadder of Nosfuckingferatu.

i was a fuckin mess an in my desperation i called Samantha up at her student digs in Sheffield an told her i wanted to come up an see her an she was like: listen, Mark, i been thinkin an you need to sort yourself out. i told you, you're headin straight for a cliff edge an if i stay w/you you're going to drag me over the edge w/you. i really like you, Mark. but i can't see you any more.

hearing her soft, methodical voice again was beautiful. but her words came like being hit in the chest w/a hammer. she was kind a cold, man. there was too much distance in her tone. i missed her an i felt totally decrepit an broken down an pathetic an i knew that this time i needed sum one, i needed her. i look at Sam an i see my past, like everything good that was ever taken away from me, it is as if it was all given back to me all wrapped up in her. but everythin was lost now, there was a certain finality in her voice an i knew i'd never see her again.

an i never did neither.

## 17

it was the bleak morning i got the letter from a friend called Turk back in L.A. 28th November 1991. i was having morning coffee an bringin myself down w/sum codeine, the morning after we'd been to see Nirvana at the Hummingbird an i got so totally fucked up again all i could remember in one vaporous moment was when Kurt Cobain threw his guitar up in the air an let it crash on the floor. otherwise, all a total blur.

the letter said Lilian had finally gone an done it. put a gun in her pretty mouth an blew her own brains out. Glock 10mm. Turk just thought i'd want to know. Jesus, Glock 10mm. must a took away half her skull. kind a left me totally frozen. it felt like everythin in my life was spinnin outta control. an i felt total regret for sum a the things i done an the things i sed. seems like sum things can only ever end a certain way an nuthin you can do an nuthin you can say will change a goddamn thing. sum times the most beautiful things in life are not meant to last, for sum reason. sum people are delicate an ephemeral like a flower, i couldn't get the haunting memory of her beautiful dark eyes out my head. we are all carrying around our own invisible scars inside us. sum times you just wonder, you just wonder if there ain't just one thing good in this world, just one thing worth livin for. but if it ain't worth livin for then it can't be worth dyin for either. but maybe it's true, maybe there's just nuthin worth caring about. i can only tell you this much: it's a tough world, there's a lot a motherfuckers in it an if you let them, they're gonna get to you.

i come to the conclusion we better off not thinking about the big issues becuz our minds just not calibrated to do it. you better off not knowing anything becuz if you don't know anything you don't have to unlearn all the crap they foisted on you. stay vacant, man. stay vacant. you were never meant to win. you're fuckin cannon fodder an the psychic warfare employed by politics is fucking up your mind an if people don't wise up to what's goin on there's gonna be sum bitter consequences.

i think people are blind, i think they just go

around w/their eyes shut an they live in the middle of a self-sufficient delusion an the people who commit suicide are the ones who can see reality for what it really is an they know, they know that monarchies sit on thrones a blud an vanquished bonedust while life for everybody is contaminated w/sum thing bad an they can see the septicity spreading an they don't wanna be part of it no more. if you go throo life just believing everythin they tell you, it's just easier that way, it's all just easier, but sum people can't do it, they can't live like that, they won't just accept all the bullshit so everythin is stacked against them.

\* \* \*

in the end, nuthin matters really. an that same night i went out w/the express intention of getting totally wrecked an i'd been to see local pub circuit band Chinky's Wig play the upstairs room at the Wheatsheaf in Walsall. they're not even bad but it's clear they just try too hard to sound like Killing Joke. they named the band after this white kid around town who's like white an all that but he looked a bit Chinese so everybody called him Chinky an his greasy black hair was cut like Mr. Spock's out a *Star Trek* so it looked like sum kinda weird shiny wig greased down on his head an he's got these slit eyes so he looks in sum way like you'd draw a cartoon Chinese face.

so as it turns out Amy's in the joint w/this scrubber kid she introduced as a friend of hers but he obviously ain't no friend, this is obviously sum other bastard she's fucking but it's no business a mine an i truly don't give a fuck an after the gig we all ended up at this kid's terraced house in a small suburb of the town called Chuckery that's like 10 or 12 miles from my own gaff. whole place is like rows an rows of old soot-blackened red brick terraced houses, i used to go to school round here an i already know the whole area is fuckin filthy an it stinks of a mixture of Pakistani cooking an weed emanating from the houses. Amy was out her skull an true to form she had that mad possessed look in her eyes when you know she's gonna pull sum lousy shit.

kid was a tall, string a piss druggy called Johnny Karidis but everyone just called him Dr. Karidis cuz of his huge stash of amphetamines an all manner of other pills i'd heard he kept in jars on shelves round his gaff so his place looked like an apothecary. i kind a knew Dr. Karidis from around but i'd never been back to his gaff an he'd never been back to mine or anythin like that, he was just one a those kids you see about all the time. but on this night after the 3 of us got tanked up on Jack Daniel's he invited me back to do some speed. he was a weird sort, got this kind a stuttering speech impediment an you really have to concentrate hard to tell anythin he's saying but his breath was like a stagnant fish-tank an i wondered to myself if there are no depths Amy wouldn't sink to. strange thing tho, he was wearing this chickenshit bright electric blue suit, an i dunno what style a suit you'd call it but it was a wide pimpin lapelled style a suit that made him look a cunt. an to top it off, the suit didn't fit him properly either, hung off his gangly frame like an old sack an it was frayed at the cuffs an round the collar like he got it from a church jumble sale or sum where.

so we wind up back at Dr. Karidis' place. it's a simple room, couple a peeling red leather sofas an a table beneath a casement window on which a teevee an VHS player sits an on the wall is a framed Joy Division poster. on the opposite wall is a decrepit looking gas fire with faux-wood veneer. it's fuckin damp an cold in the place an Karidis keeps lighting matches on the wall an spends like 10 minutes sticking them in the front a the fire while he plunges a loud clunking button on the side in an out until the fucking thing sparks into life with a loud explosion a blue flames followed by a worrying cacophonous rattle before it settles down.

his kitchen is as i'd heard - shelves lined w/sweet-shop style jars full a pills an acid tabs an Dr. Karidis calls the kitchen his laboratory. it stinks of sumthin putrid in there that he's been cookin up an whatever it is i'm pretty sure it ain't no kind a food i ever ate. but in any case for sustenance i think he might live on boiling up the rats that populate his back yard that's cluttered w/old car tyers an bits of engines an old rotting away furniture.

    we're knocking back this stomach churning cheap shit supermarket vodka which is all he keeps in an we're all sittin on the floor in his living room bombing what i thought was speed down w/the vodka but he's slipped me sum thing else that knocks me out an i wind up sprawled on the floor half conscious, drifting in an out. i lose all sensation, can't feel a thing but the last thing i see throo watery eyes is Dr. Karidis' ghost white grimacing face, his yeller teeth, an he's shootin me up in the arm, pumping me full of a cocktail of sum thing an Amy's urging him viciously: "go on, go on, give it him, give it the bastard." Dr. Karidis grins a contorted grin an says maliciously sum thing cryptic like, "time to let the genie out the bottle." an within like twenny seconds i've reached terminal velocity an it's like i hit the deck totally immobilised like i'd been hit by an express train, i'm out spread-eagled like one a those tiger rugs w/my mouth gaping open an i'm tryna move but i can't. the sense of deadness started mentally an then extended to my limbs until i couldn't feel nuthin anymore.

it was sum kind of anesthetic. i'd blacked out to the max an they left me to die an when i come to i could hear them upstairs fucking. i imagine they planned to come down in the morning an take me an dump me in the fuckin cut or sumthin an the police would a simply written me off as just another self-inflicted junky OD.

after lying on my side in a fetal position throwin my guts up on the dust-laden brown carpet i make it in a total haze crawlin to the front door, where on the telephone table i find Dr. Karidis' keys to the black Toyota HiLux that's outside an i get the fuck outta the place an take the truck w/senses gone an saliva dribbling uncontrollably from my mouth as i accelerate away. totally spaced out i leadfoot it all the way down the Birmingham Road back into the city w/the winnder rolled down tryna suck in the air an maybe there's cop cars lurkin sum where but if there is i don't see a single one but it don't matter to me at all becuz i already got it lodged in my fractured mind anyway: if one comes after me: i *ain't* stoppin. i can hear only obscure thudding abstract sounds in my ears like my head is under water an i see a morass a blurred lines as i plummet across red lights at the Scott Arms intersection, street lights burnin my retinas like napalm, veins becoming crystalised.

# 18

spent the next 2 weeks recovering after my near death experience but i hadn't seen no angels or heavenly lights at the end a no tunnel or heard no voice of no gods either, i'll tell you that. i was really just a speck a light in the eye of death, fading away.

i hadn't heard jack shit about Karidis' truck either. i left it undamaged an i walked round the corner to check on the situation an sure enough the thing had gone so i'm guessing they recovered it easy enough an Karidis got it back an nuthin else was done about it. derz no way Karidis would a wanted to take anything further, avoiding as much contact w/the law as much as possible.

i rolled out a bed an made a coffee an for the first time in days i found that i could finally start keeping stuff down.

i picked specks a mould off the bread in my cupboard an made toast. ate it dry becuz i didn't have any butter or jams or nuthin like that.

\* \* \*

"Jesus, you look skinny," Garry Barracuda sez to me as i walk in.

i tell him i've had the flu.

"he's got the AIDS," Merv looks up an says noxiously throo his rotten teeth.

i'm in the sex shop on Hurst Street buying sum VHS tapes. but i buy the under the counter stuff off Garry Barracuda who owns the place so i'm standin about waitin for Merv the Perv to finish gettin served. he's in there to buy the cheapo rubber doll he's got on the counter. but from their conversation this is like the third blow-up doll this fucking chickenshit little mutant of a man has bought in as many weeks.

"sir," Garry Barracuda sez. "perhaps you'd like me to show you a better quality one? so they last longer, er..., you know... so you don't havta keep buyin em?"

Merv the Perv's a regular in the shop an he's a really fucked-up lookin little freak who looks like Danny Devito except w/a Rod Stewart spikey kind a haircut an despite the fact he's not very tall his brown Farah trousers are too short at the ankles an he makes a stabbing action w/his fist an goes, "oooooh nooo, the quality's just fine, heh heh heh heh, it's just that... erm, heh heh heh heh heh," he checks over shoulders conspiratorily, still pumping his fist an looks up sheepishly from under his brow, "it's just that after i've fucked em i like to stab the fuck out of em." an w/that he doubles over an laughs until he turns purple an strings of saliva start hanging from his thin lips an he yanks a soiled handkerchief out his pocket to wipe his mouth, making these depraved sucking sounds.

Merv also molests little kids. he did like 5 years or sumthin for molesting a 6 year old girl up on Barr Beacon hill just near the Birmingham border with Walsall. police have bin keepin an eye on him ever since. he's banned from almost everywhere, all the parks at least. they won't have him in the library. he's got a permanent record. during the day people park up in their cars on Barr Beacon to enjoy the view. bit different of a night time tho an Merv stares at me w/his little repugnant eyes an explains, "yeah yeah, people go up there to have an ice cream, watch the wildlife an the birds an stuff. but a lot of em go up for sumthin else later on, know what i mean?" avoiding his saturnine stare i just go, "yeah yeah, i know what you mean, Merv."

"thing is," Merv the Perv sez. "it's alright for them lot to have an orgy up there but if i go up an walk about on my own the police are called an i get asked what i'm up to an dragged away. i can't even wear a pair a shorts, me. if i walk around town in the heat a summer in a pair a shorts the pigs pull me up an tell me i gotta go home an stick a pair a proper trousers on."

in silence we watch Merv leave the shop w/his new girlfriend in a bag an when the door closes behind him Garry Barracuda just shakes his head an holds out his palms an goes, "there's sumthin wrong w/him."

i nod, "he's got lowest common denominator written all over him. got my tapes?"

Garry nods an goes, "sure have, kid." an he brings the box a 5 tapes from out the back, puts it on the counter, picks out one a the tapes an goes, "brand new one here w/Angelica Bella in it," Garry winks an holds out his hand for the dosh, "that one's legit. as for the others... better not talked about. thirty quid, the lot." he drops the tape back in the box.

## 19

couple a months later back at the Hummingbird for the Sonic Youth gig. there are certain roads one must go down before we know the real value of life an i've had to go down them. as far as the life i'd chosen up until now was concerned - i had no intention of ever stopping. drugs were the best thing that ever happened to me. it has been my own personal vision quest, like American Indians. i lived life on my own terms an discovered myself throo drugs an i think all the kids should go out an do the same. me? i'd do drugs until the day i died. i never intended to stop an my feelin was that i never would neither.

you know, i don't laugh much, in fact i often look around an find myself wondering what the fuck everybody's got to laugh about. everybody's broken, man, an i got no clue why but it's like they're all smashed up an for sum reason unknown to me they're laughin at the fragments.

it was August 12th 1992. after the Sonic Youth gig. Electric an me hung around to get signatures an pass on Bob Bert's message which really made Steve Shelley laugh. as he signed my autograph book he shook his head an went, "oh, he's a bitter guy, Bob's a bitter guy."

we ambled down to the Ship Ashore to grab the last couple a drinks at last orders an i dunno what kinda weird shit night was goin down there but it weren't like it normally was, an i'm talkin about the chickenshit freakass people in the joint. place was full a street trash, no sign a the usual indie-kid crowd an the DJ's playin The Shamen's *Move Any Mountain* an watchin all those mutants dance was like the dead had risen from their graves, all dancin like they were havin sum kinda muscular spasms an while we're waitin to get served at the bar i turned to Electric an sed, "well, this is like a bus ride to shit town." course, it's all a symptom of rave culture breaking into the mainstream. the rave scene was a bit different in the 80's but now it's gone to shit like everythin always does.

we slumped down at a table in the corner in the upstairs room out the way an we're still talkin bout forming our band, The Whores of Kunt.

Electric laughed an then considered it for a moment, screwed up his mouth an sed, "Mark, that name, the Whores of Kunt, don't even mek any sense."

"nuthin ever does," i told him, "nuthin ever does."

sitting just across from us were 2 skanky looking old birds who looked like Bette Davis an Joan Crawford in *Whatever Happened to Baby Jane?* their haggard faces sagged in melancholy hollowness an both of them just sat an stared pretty much catatonic, staring at a fixed point in space at sum thing i couldn't see. but i knew that what they were staring into was the bottomless void of their own desolate lives.

the walls i've constructed around myself mean nobody really knows me. my relationships are all surface relationships an sum time in the future maybe when i'm older i'll feel sad that i didn't ever take time to look into the deeper soul of anyone or open mine to them or maybe i am simply physiologically unable to. sum times i wonder if i have the capacity to truly love at all. i wonder if i am incapable of it an always just go throo a series of behaviours that just got a semblance of it. maybe i just weren't born the right way. all those nights as a kid alone in the dark, heart just about beating, all desires already forgotten an just about kissed goodbye to all dreams i ever once might a had. comes on you like a sickness, like a cancer of the mind, a cancer of the soul. you're always surrounded but always alone.

for sure you've seen me drifting around all over the city, zonked out in all the bars an clubs, you seen me walking the streets, an down in the subways. you seen me in the train stations an the cafés, you seen me buyin my vinyl in Reddingtons Rare Records an the Plastic Factory an in Swordfish Records an the Diskery. you seen me down Hurst Street in the Razor's Edge buyin my old 501's an beaten up vintage clothes. you seen me strung out my mind watching all those bands at all those gigs. you seen me, an yet you never really noticed me an you do not know me. i am the nobody man, swallowed up by it all.

Electric an me got turfed out the Ship Ashore at about 1 a.m. we staggered down Digbeth to a greasy kebab joint an stood outside the place eating our greasy kebabs strobed in flashing blue light from 3 police riot vans parked diagonally on the road as cops dealt w/sum kinda drunken mass brawl spreadin out across the pavements, street lights orange above. near us a cop got a kid in an armlock down on the floor an sum other kid w/bright ginger hair sittin cross-legged on the pavement, his back against the wall, drinkin a bottle a Bud, watchin the action while goin *da de du du deeee deeeerrr* doin the theme from *Hawaii 5-0* laughs an shouts, "book'em, Danno!"

* * *

following morning i got the shakes bad an even a smoke a grass couldn't assuage it. so i'm back down the Melancholy Café gettin a fried breakfast w/a wizened up face like Neil Kinnock sucking snake venom out a Margaret Thatcher's a-hole. an i gotta laugh becuz en route walking down to the joint, on the corner of Inge Street i see Big D the dwarf out an about, bright as a button like he ain't got a care in the world. i got no idea what kind a goldbrick he's tryna pull on everybody this time but he's wearin a cowboy hat an he's got sum kind a collecting bucket that people are tossing coins into. he's still in his massive, baggy cargo shorts/trousers but he's also wearin a *Nuke Em High* sweatshirt like he's actually 1 a the mutants out the film, his greasy hair flying about around his ears in the wind. man, he's another 1 who's got *lowest common denominator* written all over him, may as well have it tattooed across his forehead. but good old Big D, doesn't give a flying fuck about nuthin. you gotta give it the little poison dwarf, he's totally unstoppable. looks happy as a lark, pullin his shit.

i was always a lonely boy, just drifting around this world like sum dark, unidentifiable abstract shape. i was fucked-up from day one. born fucked-up. an no matter what anyone did could a changed a damn thing about the fact. but i will unequivocally tell you this: i don't give a fuck bout anythin. an you can say whatever you want to say as you waste away your lives in your offices or on your factory production lines, punching your clock in an out every day. fuck that. society is an idiocracy. i will not succumb. i will not succumb. i will not succumb. an i don't care if it kills me, at least i got the guts. at least i can say w/all conviction i got the guts to live the way i wanna live an do the things i wanna do. an we, we are the narcotic generation, the generation that finally found our escape. an now that we have: how does society like its wide-eyed boys?

an i'll tell you this as well. i'll never accept no religion neither. when you got a political leader who goes an claims they're acting under the auspices of God or Allah or whatever the hell they wanna call it then you got a fuckin problem. a big fuckin problem. an you got a problem w/all these converted fuckers running about the streets. these people are out there an religion is a complete personality transplant.

there's sum people probably think i'm just sum loused up anarchist. but i ain't no anarchist, i ain't no nuthin. truth is i simply see socialism as the personification of evil. society is being suppressed by socialist tyranny an these kids need a new kind a rock n roll, a new form a youth movement. they all need a good punch up the knickers, an they need to start having fun again to free them from all this beehive politics that's being engendered; the state being the queen bee we all work an subsequently die for. fuck politicians an fuck governments an fuck the priests an their churches. to me, socialists an religionists are one an the same kinda ideologue. they're villains. they're the real villains in society. fuck em all up the ass w/a red-hot poker. their creed ain't no creed a mine. wish i could just wipe them all away like the disease they are.

i tell you what i think. i think they're just a bunch a self-indulgent moral crusaders hiding their real machinations behind a veneer a morality. but such nuanced thinkers ain't got no real political theory, they just throw in a load a bullshit words an phrases, their politics is nuthin but a quasi-religion. but the effective truth is human nature never really alters

but me, i have to record these things. i have to record them becuz these are the lives we led, an these were the things we seen an the things we heard. an if we don't record them, the powers that be will write any version a history they like, make it like we never existed at all, not even for a single moment, like this society died in entropy an that just ain't true at all. we must tear down monarchies an their palaces, the false facades of society becuz a politicised society is a contaminated society wherein all the dumbfucks got their core-selves supplanted by ideaologies an all their bullshit an perjury becomes the official version a history.

well, at least i can hold my head high an say even if i failed at least i tried, at least i tried to beat the system. at least i fuckin tried to apply my own cognitive thoughts to the disinformation they tried to feed me, an i can say that i saw throo all the smoke an mirrors.

at the end a the day, as i see it, we ain't doin much wrong. it's all a sick an sinister game an i hope when i look back on it all i'll remember us this way: that we were just a bunch a kids wiling away our days while we were still young enough to do it. an we were just tryna not get pulled into the fixed order a things that's soley set up to systematically destroy individuals. but all these chickenshits don't think w/enough complexity about how these fuckin governments want to equalize society until everythin becomes political thought an people gotta stop being so god-damn blind becuz once your thoughts are politicised an not your own they got you by the balls. they say in life you need a backbone but you don't necessarily need no backbone when you got a middle finger.

what an absolute can a worms, man. an i've heard it sed that all this is pure fabrication. an you too might be all incredulous an say these things never happened but i don't give 2 fucks about your views. an i don't know what kind a world you live in right now or what your future cities will look like. i dunno what shape your social mores will take. or what kinda horse shit your government's gonna be tryna hawk you. but this was my world. at least for a little while it was.

we are all just trapped in our own short life spans. these are just sum a my memories from these days, an although you an i can never meet across the vast spectrum of time an one day both me an this world i knew will be sunk into the abyss like a stone, these things happened in Birmingham City in the early 1990's. we lived all the deth an destruction an hopelessness of these things cuz we had nuthin else to live for an in the end there was just nuthin else to die for neither. but at least i can say in all truth i never played their bullshit game an i never let them cut my heart out. but sum times i succeeded in cutting out theirs. an it was fun doing it while it lasted. it was fun doing it. an know this for evermore - that when my time comes an i'm in my dying moments, my final thoughts will be this: i never once became the adherent a no creed, an i never swallowed the bullshit. i never swallowed the bullshit.

but one day just like other species that have been before us human beings will become extinct an nuthin gonna matter one bit. becuz every body's goin around sleepwalkin into sum thing an i dunno what it is they're sleepwalkin into but i will tell you this much: everyone's thoughts are contaminated w/politics an they're gonna start thinkin only in allegories an whatever it is we're all heading for, it's gonna be sumthin bad. it's gonna be sumthin really bad.

the skies are grey.
the air is lukewarm.
the city all around me is operating at temperate speed an volume.
everything is nondescript.
it's like sum illusion that's keeping everybody sleepwalking into the advancing cataclysm.


sum short-haired blonde kid wearing a pristine white Levi's Sta-Press jacket is in the Melancholy Café an he's just sittin there w/his feet up on the adjacent seat, staring throo mirror shades lookin cool like he thinks he's Steve fuckin McQueen or sum body. he's drinkin a glass a milk throo a stripey straw like the old *watch out there's a Humphrey about*

Unigate Milk teevee advert when i was a kid where the Humphrey milk thieves stole your milk throo stripey straws.

you can smell the burnt toast an the cookin oil from the saucepans bubbling on the fume blackened hobs an i'm gettin a can from the Coke machine. On the front a the machine it says in big white letters:

**COKE ADDS LIFE.**

i slot in my coins an stab the button. the machine makes a clunking sound but nuthin happens, "hey, Darkie," i shout. "it hasn't given me my Coke!"

"nah. it's busted," Darkie says disinterestedly, not even lookin at me, wiping his greasy palms on the front of his chef's apron.

"well stick a fucking sign on it or sumthin then why don't you?" i tell him, sitting back down in my chair.

# 20

i got sum top notch speed an i'm in the toilets at Loaded on a Saturday night, locked in 1 a the cubicles. i shoot up in the wrist an just discard my rig down the toilet pan. i sit on the toilet w/the lid down an read a poem sum lefty socialist scratched on the partitian wall w/a knife:

## **REVOLUTION**

**grow some balls.
if the government shoves razorblades
down yr throat
you gonna say thank you
just because yr starving?**

i come to the conclusion the human race ain't exactly evil. we're all collectively locked into sum kind a self annihilation, like we're pre-programed to self terminate an there's nuthin no one can do about it. the human race is hurtling towards sum abominable ending, total annihilation on a sub-atomic level.

it takes couple a mins for the speed to reach my brain an then the sheer violence of the hit is like an express train straight throo my skull.
i suck in air.

30 minutes later back in the club, the speed full on pumping throo my veins. last time i saw Electric he was fucked up near the food-bar, not buying any food just half-comatose over the counter but now i've lost him sumwhere around an i'm at the bar alone, sum smiling

bugged-out kid w/dyed blue hair i never seen before is saying sumthin enthusiastically right in my face an although i smile back an nod i can't tell a word he sez over 999's *Homicide* blasting out the sound system. cigarette smoke hangs in the air between us.

i go over to the DJ's booth an ask him if he got any Cramps an he goes yeah yeah sure an promises he'll play sum but i'm so amped up an caught in a haze i don't even recognise it even if he ever does an i'm just walking around the club watchin it all goin on an all i can feel is the massive amalgamation a noizes an visions overloading my senses an my whole body is on edge, tingling.

wrecking on the dancefloor lights an the music just goin blam blam blam blam an the blud's pulsing throo my quickened arteries, my heartbeat hammering like a 1000 miles an hour an i am twisting, turning, spinning, swirling, screaming, throwing out my arms in abandon an i just wanna get a gun an blow the stars out the sky.

my head's about to explode. i'm in a fervid cold sweat, grinding my teeth to stubs, an i take a moment a serenity to cool down out in the foyer, kick back on the sofa an spark up a cigarette. bass drum a Blondie's *Dreaming* comes pounding throo the walls an throo the floor. but i'm scared the hit might wear off so i do a bit of a dab from a wrap in my pocket, sour on my tongue. the bored brunette at the pay-in booth whispers sumthin no doubt caustic about me to 1 a the bouncers, she nods subtly in my direction but i don't move or even bat an eyelid as the goon eyeballs me suspiciously but he don't do nuthin an after a bit i douse my cigarette in the ashtray an get up an head back in the club.

for i don't know how long i sit alone on a black leather armchair in the corner gripping a Jack Daniel's, watching people making angular shapes like a series a dazzling images throo the blankets a dry ice captured in camera flash strobe lights.

sum long-haired kid in a Pixies tshirt briefly comes over an sits on the arm a the chair, rolls a cigarette on his knee, puts it between his lips, smiles at me an walks away. i can't see anything w/any normal regularity, it's like my eyes are just taking photographs, snap snap snap snap an freezing each frame, i'm just an observer, recording moments in time.

afterwards, back out on the street, my Cuban heels striking the pavements at 4 a.m everythin looks sparse an white, the city pulsing around me to the soundtrack feedbacking in my head. blast of sparkling city lights against indigo early mornin sky. dark tower blocks. cold winds squalling throo deserted cinereal subways.

big kid in a black Sex Gang Children tshirt worn under a leather trench coat w/cigarette stickin out his mouth stops me an asks for a light. the epochal click of the Zippo lid. i spark him up. "nice night for a stroll," he says as he walks away.

still not quite at baseline yet, my fuses totally blown, i'm drained a blud, detached from my surroundings, experiencing only plastic sensations. everythin around me looks like the monochrome colours of a negative photograph, as if i'm seeing in infra-red.

i walk up to St. Philip's Place an sit on a bench in the shadder a the cathedral, waitin for the sun to come up. as far as i know, the planets are still revolving around the sun.

old newspapers blowing around in the wind. my body feels calm now, a kind a breathe easy tranquility creeping over me. every now an again tiny electric sparks of pinhole light detonate in my retinas. i'm watching shootin stars across the sky. i've never felt more alive.

sum beautiful wasted girl w/pink hair an sad brown eyes wearing a short skirt who looks like Pris out a *Blade Runner* wanders over from out a nowhere an sits down on the bench. i pull a couple a Marlboros out my crumpled softpack an crash her 1.

"where you bin?" the girl says as i light her up w/my Zippo.

"Loaded," i tell her.

"ah!" she goes. "indie-boy, eh?"

"yeah. bout you?"

"bin up Coast to Coast, she says wryly. "i'm a barmaid. i spend my nights smiling at people i'd rather kick in the face."

"only bin up there once," i say. "it aint my scene 1 bit. all like house music or sumthin."

"just work there." the girl shrugs. "not my kinda place either. i sing in a band though. that's really my thing."

"yeah? what's your band called?"

"Kill Hard Kill Fast."

"oh, that's a cool name," i say. "i'm starting a band. the Whores of Kunt."
the girl laughs. "that name doesn't make any sense," she sez. i shake my head. so it goes, i tell the girl. so it goes.

the sky starts to get a bit bluer. looking up at the heavens i say, "i love watching the stars fade away in the morning, don't you?" the girl nods thoughtfully an goes, "yeah... like angels in apprehension. too afraid of this world to come down here. an who can blame em?"

"not me," i shake my head. "not me."

we sit in silence for a while just smokin our cigarettes an watching the starlings start to come out the trees an peck for worms in the dewed grass. the girl swivels herself round to face me an goes: "how about this then?" inexplicably she lifts up her top revealing her perfectly formed small breasts an i just stare all kinda surprised, like a stupid rabbit in headlights an the girl rolls her eyes an sez, "*feeel*, dumbass."

i caress her breast, feel the hardness of her dark red nipple. she watches my hand move down her transluscent white body, over her delicate ribs. she's breathing lightly, gently pressing herself into my hand. then w/out any further elaboration she just gets up, throws her cigarette stub to the floor an crushes it under her foot. she straightens up her top, smiles deliberately an says..."see ya." an walks away.

i shout "hey wait" but she either don't hear or just flat out ignores me.

man, i thought i'd seen sum things but that just about takes the biscuit. city of millions a strangers is pretty much the lonliest place you can be. i just sit joylessly an watch the girl walk away. w/out looking back at all she crosses Cathedral Square onto Colmore Row an like sum kind a ghost she fades away into the distance out my life forever. i want to run after her but that would be a bit pathetic. she disappears down Church Street out of view an it's as if she never existed at all.

2 angels peer down at the earth. 1 called Ignatious W. Crumb an the other called Millicent Macuish. an Millicent Macuish sez: "but how did all these human beings get down there?" an Ignatious W. Crumb throws out his palms an he says to her kind of exasperated, he says: "don't you get it? they're all *born* down there. an they grow stupid down there throo lack of any aspirations. so they eke out their pitiful existence down there until the day they die an after all that, after everything they subject themselves to, they're simply buried in the earth down there."

"won't they ever learn the full nature of their potential?" Millicent Macuish asks.

"they don't have any potential. they're not as we are," Ignatious W. Crumb explains tonelessly. "they're all ugly dullards whose egos are such they choose to believe they're aligned with us angels as opposed to the brutish apes from whom they are truly descended."

"how long do these apes live?"

"individually they only live for a short time, almost happily in the quagmire of shit of their own making. even as a species it's been written in their dna to self destruct. their existence is ultimately pointless an futile an on a universal scale as we angels know it, their whole duration is the blink of an eye."

"we can't help improve them?" Millicent Macuish wonders.

"nah, fuck 'em," Ignatious W. Crumb shrugs dispassionately. "it was all an experiment gone to crap. 1 day soon their ugly pallid faces will all be gone."

## 21

the city is coming to life again as the 2 remaining stars dissolve in the sky. an of course, there are no gods an no angels in the heavens. it's all pure invention. it's all pure invention an no body's going to convince me of anythin to the contrary an everybody got to stop blaming everybody else for our misfortunes an our stupid transgressions becuz we are all miniscule. we are miniscule in the grand order a things an if this whole planet went kablooey right now the universe an everythin that might be in it would just impartially carry on expanding. it don't care about us, we ain't no children of no gods. we're on our own, man.

but i will tell you this much: if we can imagine gods, we can be gods. if we can imagine gods, we can *be* gods. we can be gods an at the end a your life you gotta be able to say in all truth i never once let anyone tell me what to do, an i never once let anyone tell me what to think. an sum people have sed i'm out a control. but truth is i never let any body mould me, i never let any body shape me into what they wanted me to be. an at least i can damn well say that an i'll be tellin the truth, too.

it's 5.30 a.m. my joints are stiff from the cold now an i begin the slow walk home.

protruding above diaphanous folds of mist the red light on top a the monolithic Post Office Tower flashes resolutely.

**END.**

# Murder Slim Press: Checklist

- MSP#000 – *The Savage Kick #1* ft. Dan Fante ☐
- MSP#001 – *Hating Olivia* by Mark SaFranko ☐
- MSP#002 – *Role of A Lifetime* by Mark SaFranko ☐
- MSP#003 – *The Savage Kick #2* ft. Doug Stanhope ☐
- MSP#004 – *The Savage Kick #3* ft. Jim Goad ☐
- MSP#005 – *Steps* by Steve Hussy ☐
- MSP#006 – *The Angel* by Tommy Trantino ☐
- MSP#007 – The Savage Kick #4 ft. Joe Matt ☐
- MSP#008 – *Lounge Lizard* by Mark SaFranko ☐
- MSP#009 – *Loners* by Mark SaFranko ☐
- MSP#010 – *Life Change* by Mark SaFranko ☐
- MSP#011 – *Savage Kick #5* by Mark SaFranko ☐
- MSP#012 – *The Hunch* by Seymour Shubin ☐
- MSP#013 – *God Bless America* by Mark SaFranko ☐
- MSP#014 – *Lonely No More* by Seymour Shubin ☐
- MSP#015 – *The Savage Kick #6* ft. Debbie Drechsler ☐
- MSP#016 – *NAM* by Robert McGowan ☐
- MSP#017 – *A Long Perambulation* by Robert McGowan ☐
- MSP#018 – *We Are Glass* by u.v. ray ☐
- MSP#019 – *Bank Blogger* by Jeffrey P. Frye ☐
- MSP#020 – *Why Me?* by Seymour Shubin ☐
- MSP#021 – *One Crazy Day* by Jeffrey P. Frye ☐
- MSP#022 – *Spiral Out* by u.v. ray ☐
- MSP#023 – *Dirty Work* by Mark SaFranko ☐
- MSP#024 – *The Captain* by Seymour Shubin ☐
- MSP#025 – *The Savage Kick #7* ft. Carson Mell ☐
- MSP#026 – *The Migrant* by u.v. ray ☐
- MSP#027 – *Back* by Steve Hussy ☐
- MSP#028 – *Sometimes You Just...* by Mark SaFranko ☐
- MSP#029 – *The Artistic Life* by Mark SaFranko ☐
- MSP#030 – *South Main Stories* by Robert McGowan ☐
- MSP#031 – *Black Cradle* by u.v. ray ☐
- MSP#032 – *Saint Of The City* by David Noone ☐
- MSP#033 – *The Savage Kick #8* ft. Cathi Unsworth ☐
- MSP#034 – *The Savage Kick #9* ft. Mark SaFranko ☐
- MSP#035 – *Blossoms and Blood* by Mark SaFranko ☐
- MSP#036 – *The Savage Kick #10* ft. Willy Vlautin ☐
- MSP#037 – *Drug Story* by u.v. ray ☐
- MSP#038 – *Little Miss Awesome* by Steve Hussy ☐
- MSP#039 – *Little Miss Awesome* by Ally North ☐

# murder slim press

since 2004

*writing at the razor's edge*

murderslim.com

Printed in Great Britain
by Amazon